# AFTER THE FIRE

**Visit us at www.boldstrokesbooks.com**

# By the Author

Searching For Forever

Same Time Next Week

After the Fire

# AFTER THE FIRE

*by*

Emily Smith

2016

**AFTER THE FIRE**
© 2016 By Emily Smith. All Rights Reserved.


ISBN 13: 978-1-62639-652-4

This Trade Paperback Original Is Published By
Bold Strokes Books, Inc.
P.O. Box 249
Valley Falls, NY 12185

First Edition: March 2016

---

**CREDITS**
Editor: Shelley Thrasher
Production Design: Susan Ramundo
Cover Design By Melody Pond

# Chapter One

Connor Haus didn't like firefighters. She respected them, sure. She was, after all, among the majority who found themselves wanting to run from the burning building, not toward it. They were brave, and strong, and heroic. But Connor also found them arrogant and foolish—not exactly ideal qualities when it came to saving lives. And saving lives was all Connor really cared about anymore.

Her partner of the last ten years, a young, energetic EMT with a boyish smile named Jake O'Harrigan, slammed the ambulance into park, but she was already hanging out the open passenger side door, ready to leap to her feet as soon as the rig came to a stop.

"Meet you there." She grabbed the massive gear bag from the back and rushed to the woman sitting on the curb, leaving Jake behind to haul the stretcher. Boston Fire Department was on scene first. Of course they were. Although, for the life of her, Connor could never understand why the system operated that way. Firefighters, to her, were good for one thing, and that was brutish work like spraying hundreds of gallons of water onto high-rises or cutting people out of cars. The city required that most of them be trained in some level of emergency medical services, but to Connor, medicine, especially street medicine, should be left to the paramedics.

"Nice of you guys to join us." A rosy-cheeked man-child the size of a small house was holding an oxygen mask to the young woman's face while he smirked mercilessly at Connor. She knew him. She knew most of them. His name was Marty Taylor, and he was one of the many members of BFD who fueled her hatred and often irrational irritation toward the profession.

"I'll take it from here, Taylor." But Marty didn't move. "I said we've got this."

"If you're interested, this is Meg. She called us for difficulty breathing. Respirations are 32, pulse is 120, alert and oriented times four. History of asthma."

Connor dropped her bag and zeroed in on her patient. Before she'd even seen Taylor, she'd noted the girl's pallor and the icy tint to her lips and under her sunken eyes. She looked sick. It was an insight, or more a sense, that Connor had finely tuned over her ten years as a medic. She couldn't explain it, really, and she certainly couldn't teach anyone how to do it. But whatever it was, Connor knew it. And this woman was sick.

"O2 sat?" She was greeted with silence while she felt for a pulse on the patient's clammy wrist. "Taylor? What was her sat when you got here?" She gave him a cool glance.

"I...I guess I didn't get one—"

"What do you mean you didn't get a sat?"

"I forgot...She's on four liters on the mask though." This was why Connor couldn't stand firefighters who tried to play medic. Most of the guys she'd encountered had been just like Taylor, too, quick to be the hero but missing key pieces of the puzzle so crucial when it came to life or death. She said nothing but unzipped the front pocket of the bag and pulled out the pulse oximeter.

"86 percent. Damn it." She looked back up at the pale face in front of her. "Meg? My name is Connor. I'm a paramedic. Can you tell me what happened?"

The young woman on the curb forced a small smile through the plastic oxygen mask, but her color was getting worse by the minute. If Connor didn't do something, fast, she'd have to intubate.

"Have...asthma..." She gasped. "Can't...breathe..."

Jake showed up next to them with the stretcher in tow.

"Just relax. We're going to help you. Jake, can you put together an albuterol treatment for me? And quickly?"

Connor cranked the oxygen tank up to eight and watched the numbers on the oximeter. They weren't budging. Taylor stood up, pacing uncomfortably back and forth, the thudding of his heavy black boots on the frozen Jamaica Plain pavement echoing in Connor's ears. While she waited, she helped the woman slowly to her feet, neither Jake nor Taylor offering much in the way of assistance, and sat her down on the ambulance stretcher. Finally, Taylor ran off, returning with a wool blanket, which he proudly wrapped around her shoulders.

"Here you go, Boss." Jake handed her a breathing treatment, which she quickly placed in the woman's mouth.

"This is albuterol, just like what's in your inhaler, only stronger. Just breathe normally, okay? We'll get you feeling better in no time." Her voice was strong and confident, but inside, like always, she was writhing. Connor thought back to an instructor she'd had in paramedic school who was always telling her to "be the duck"—flailing under the water to stay afloat but calm on the surface. She'd found she was quite good at being the duck. And no matter how hot things got, Connor knew how to pretend they weren't. Jake, on the other hand, wasn't quite as gifted in this area. He joined Taylor in his pacing until Connor was sure the two of them were going to wear holes in their shoes. *This must be why those idiots wear rubber boots.*

Within a few minutes, the young woman's cheeks transformed from a frigid white to a delicate pink, her lips no longer reminding Connor of a 7-11 Slurpee drink. The numbers on the oximeter climbed, slowly, until they reached 92—a reading she could live with, and so could her patient.

"How are you feeling now?" she asked, placing her stethoscope to the woman's back.

"So much better. I can breathe...Thank you. You're a lifesaver."

Connor smiled at her. "That's sort of the idea."

Taylor motioned to his buddy, who'd been sitting on the back of the engine playing on his cell phone through the entire series of events. Connor thought she'd actually prefer it if everyone in BFD just stayed with their truck. That way they couldn't bother her or her patients.

"Let's get her loaded up for Haus here, shall we?"

The two spry men in their bunker gear effortlessly lifted the woman and the stretcher into the back of the Boston EMS rig. At least they're good for one thing, Connor thought. I'll probably be able to work into my sixties without a back injury. She grinned to herself and hopped into the ambulance.

By the time Jake pulled into the ambulance bay at Boston City Hospital, the young woman was telling Connor about her three dachshunds at such length that you'd have had to wonder if she'd ever been sick at all.

This was her favorite part of the job—finding them in crisis and bringing them in fixed. Jake yanked open the heavy back doors, and the two of them lowered the stretcher to the ground and walked through the emergency room. A blast of heat reminded Connor that it was still January in Massachusetts. She rarely noticed things like the weather while she worked, though. Even in her thin Boston EMS fleece and cargo pants, she'd been sweating under the heat of death right in front of her.

"Connor. You brought us a present." Galen Burgess, the young ER resident with California-blond hair and a year-long tan met them at the door.

"Anything for you, Galen." Connor gave her an overt wink and a smile.

"Welcome. I'm Dr. Burgess, the resident on today. I'll be taking care of you."

"Hi. I'm Meg."

Galen followed Connor and Jake down the hall and into one of the exam rooms, where she took the woman's arm and guided her to the bed.

Galen Burgess embodied sex, and she knew it. Every woman who came through the Boston City ER when she was on staff was immediately swept up in her West Coast charm and toothy smile. When they met two years earlier, Connor had vowed not to be one of the many women on Galen's list of conquests. But in a few months Galen had cornered her in an on-call room with a bottle of chardonnay and a few smooth lines. Connor was helpless. They'd slept together several more times before Galen disappeared, Connor eventually finding her in the arms of one of the maternity nurses behind a curtain in Room 4.

It had taken a solid year before she could look at Galen without wanting to find the nearest emesis basin. But she was finally over it. Galen Burgess was fun, and sexy, and dangerous, and they enjoyed the mutual flirtation whenever Connor brought Galen a patient. But that was it. And that worked out just fine for Connor. She wasn't interested in anything even resembling a relationship. Not with Galen and not with anyone.

❖

The radio on Connor's hip remained unusually quiet, so she took just a moment to say good-bye to Galen and her patient, and swing by the cafeteria for a much-needed coffee. With her thirty-second birthday a few weeks away, she was getting a little old to be working 24-hour shifts. And as she filled a paper cup with the hot coffee, she thought briefly about getting off the streets.

She could go back to school to be a nurse, or even a physician assistant. But she liked the streets.

She even loved them. She loved the rush of being the first to find a patient who was sick or hurt. She loved making people better with only what was in her gear bag or on her truck. She loved bunking with Jake in the station on their long stretches together. Connor would never leave. She'd be a paramedic until she died or retired—whichever came first.

A clumsy hand smudged with black soot reached over her for the creamer, knocking Connor's hot coffee all over her front.

"Really?" Connor grumbled, grabbing a stack of napkins and patting herself down.

"I'm so sorry…"

She finally looked up, irate about having to go back out into the cold in a coffee-stained uniform because some dumb-ass lug of a firefighter couldn't wait his turn for the Half and Half. But the owner of the clumsy hand wasn't a "he" at all, although she might not have noticed if she hadn't looked closely. This person wore yellow bunker pants and a gray T-shirt damp with sweat around her back and chest. Her chin-length hair was pulled back into a ponytail, and her chiseled face was brushed with more black along her strong cheeks.

"BFD. Figures." Connor glared into the woman's bold, blue eyes.

"Excuse me?"

"Nothing."

"At least let me go find you a pair of scrubs," the woman offered.

"No. You've done enough for today, thanks."

Connor went back to fruitlessly dabbing the growing stains on her jacket that seeped through to her polo shirt. They stopped at her Kevlar, but it was going to be a miserable sixteen hours until she could shower and change. With any luck, she and Jake would make it back to the station long enough to find a new shirt in the boss's office. But luck wasn't something she often depended on.

"Suit yourself." The woman brushed off Connor's dismissal and skipped out of the cafeteria to meet her fellow clumsy, dumb-ass firefighter buddies.

"What are you still doing here? And what's that fragrance you're wearing today? Eau de espresso?"

Connor had waited for Galen outside an exam room, where Galen was tenderly pressing on a small child's belly and laughing with her parents.

"I don't want to talk about it…" Connor's handheld crackled to life with a jarring tone she'd know anywhere. "Shit."

"Medic 884, respond to 29 Tower Street for a 3-alpha-10. Ninety-two-year-old female with chest pain. Over." She grabbed the radio from its holster.

"884 to ops. Anyone else to take this one? I've had a bit of a fight with a cup of coffee and was hoping to make it back to base to change. Over."

"No can do, 884. All other units are out. Sorry. Over."

Connor groaned and rolled her eyes. "884 responding. Over."

"You can't go outside in that."

"Think you can get me some scrubs?"

Galen nodded and rushed to a supply closet around the corner, retrieving matching blue pants and a top even thinner than the coffee-stained clothes she already wore. At least she'd be dry. Connor silently cursed the woman from the cafeteria again under her breath.

"I owe you." She kissed Galen quickly on the cheek.

"I'll remember that!"

"Pig."

❖

Jake was waiting in the driver's seat for her when she arrived back in the ambulance bay.

"What happened to you?"

"Fucking BFD happened to me."

"You're going to wear those?" he asked, obviously incredulous.

"Better than looking like I should be collecting change in Downtown Crossing."

"You know," Jake flipped on the lights and sirens and peeled out of the Boston City parking lot, "you really have to drop this grudge against BFD. They aren't all bad."

"Just drive, Jake."

Connor stripped down to her bra and panties while Jake weaved through busy Boston traffic. Although many of the guys considered Connor hot—beautiful, even—he'd stopped gawking years ago, when he realized he liked having Connor as an upgraded version of his bitchy, unapproachable older sister better. Still, most people would say she was gorgeous, with long dancer's legs and eyelashes for miles. They would also say that Connor was definitely gay, and not just weekend, drunk-party gay, like Jake had hoped when they first were paired off together. No, Connor had no more interest in being with men than she did in being with wild gorillas. That didn't stop the newest members of Boston EMS from trying, though. Or the BFD, for that matter. But Connor was quick to offer a witty let-down with a clear message of "never going to happen," and that was always the end of that.

"I'm totally serious, Haus. One of these days you're going to have to stop thinking that everyone who rides on an engine is exactly like Kam."

Connor felt her brow drop into a frown as she wiggled to get the scrub pants over her curvy hips. "My feelings about BFD have absolutely nothing to do with her."

"Is that right?"

"Completely."

"I don't believe that for a second." Jake wailed the siren one more time as if for emphasis.

"I don't care if you believe it or not."

"Sure you do." Jake turned the rig off the main strip through the busy Jamaica Plain neighborhood. "Before Kam, you loved firefighters. Even Taylor."

"Not true."

"Yes. It is. Those guys are our brothers. And if you don't lose this grudge, you'll never be the medic you used to be."

Connor leapt from the front seat as soon as she was safely able, her boots sliding on the ice where she landed.

"This conversation isn't over, Haus!"

She smiled and loaded the bag and the portable heart monitor onto the stretcher, pulling it toward the house.

❖

Connor loved to be able to completely clear her mind of absolutely everything else while she worked. It was why she picked up those extra shifts that kept her out on the truck for what was almost two days straight at times. She didn't have to think about her life. And she never had to be lonely. She never had to think about Kam.

Unfortunately, though, Connor couldn't work every minute of every day, although she'd certainly tried to find ways. She hated this time of day—the end of her shift, when she'd wipe down all the gear in the rig, collect her things, and take the T back to her tiny studio in Cambridge, alone. More often than not, Jake would invite her to have dinner with him and his wife, but they had a new baby at home, and besides, Connor usually wasn't great company.

Instead, she'd take the stairs to her dusty apartment, feed the cat, boil a pot of water for boxed pasta, and sit in front of a

Netflix marathon. It wasn't a terrible life. She was able to afford a decent place, had a few friends in the area, and at the very least, got to immerse herself in the adrenaline and drama of the job. Most of the time, she was able to get by without thinking too much about Kam. But not that night.

Jake had pulled out the stitches of her still-healing wound, exposing her to the pain she'd become so good at avoiding. Her cat, Rusty, curled up in the crook left by her legs while she flipped mindlessly through the channels on the television. It took a while, but she'd finally managed to forget that Rusty hadn't started out as hers. Connor actually hated cats. "Some kind of lesbian you are," Kam used to joke. But Rusty had grown on her, even won her heart. Kam had loved that damn cat more than anything, even celebrating his birthday by buying him a new toy and a can of wet food every year. Connor told her that she knew better than to ever make Kam choose between her and the cat, because she'd lose every time.

As if reading her thoughts, Rusty jumped off the couch and trotted to the helmet and bunker jacket still hanging from the coat rack, then rubbed under the hem, purring so loudly Connor could hear him from across the room. The captain of Kam's unit had shown up at their door a week after it happened, holding a box with the gear.

"I thought you might want to have this," he'd said. Connor's eyes were instantly so flooded with tears she could no longer make him out. She nodded graciously and, not knowing what else to do with them, hung them on the rack, as if Kam were still there—as if she'd be coming home.

## Chapter Two

Y ou look like hell," Jake said as Connor made her way through the station to their rig.

"Oh, that's nice."

"I just call it like I see it. Everything okay?"

"Huh? Oh, sure. Just didn't sleep much last night."

Connor opened the back doors to the ambulance and began checking their equipment while Jake stood by watching.

"I meant what I said yesterday, Haus. You have to get over this Kam thing and start getting along with BFD. It's starting to make me look bad."

"Well, God forbid I make Jake O'Harrigan, EMT Basic, look bad to the other units."

"Low blow. You know I'm going to paramedic school next fall. Don't be harping on my rank."

Connor's face warmed. "You're right. Sorry."

"Look, I'm not saying you should forget about Kam. None of us will ever forget about her. She made a judgment call. A bad one. You can't hold that against every firefighter you meet. But most of all, you have to forgive her."

She stopped what she was doing and stared at Jake, anger and anguish washing over her. She wanted to pummel him for making her think about Kam. She'd done just fine for the past three years, going on as if nothing had happened. Or, at least, she was surviving. And now her punk-ass partner felt like playing therapist for the day. She didn't want to think about Kam. She thought about her enough as it was. For Christ sake, she still lived in their apartment. The place was like a shrine. Or, really, more like a tomb. Kam's medals still hung on the wall. Her sneakers still sat in the hall closet. Their names were still posted on the buzzer outside. Some people found it easier to cleanse their lives of any reminders. Connor found it best to just pretend like nothing had changed.

For her eighteenth birthday, Connor's parents had paid for her to take her basic EMT course. While most kids were getting cars and computers, Connor wanted nothing more than to learn how to extricate someone from a vehicle and take a blood pressure. Kam had been the first person she saw when she walked into the classroom that night—or she was at least the first person she noticed. How could anyone not notice her? She was tall, with the broadest shoulders Connor had ever seen. She wore a Red Sox cap over wavy brown hair that hung in strands down the back of her neck and talked effortlessly with one of the boys sitting next to her. Connor had instantly never wanted anyone more.

"Haus? Did you hear me?" Jake tossed a box of rubber gloves at her, breaking into her daydream.

"Yeah. I heard you."

"I don't think you did. You act like you've moved on, but you haven't. Instead, you take it out on everyone on BFD. You want to honor Kam's memory, treat these guys the way she did. Punishing them won't bring her back."

"I honor Kam's memory every goddamn day. And how dare you suggest otherwise. You're way out of line, O'Harrigan. Why don't you try something new and get to work." Connor turned gruffly back to the checklist in front of her. Jake was right about one thing, at least. Kam would be downright pissed if she saw the way Connor had begun to treat her brothers. Especially Marty Taylor. Taylor had been Kam's best friend. He was her Jake.

Connor had shared countless bottles of beer with Taylor and his girlfriend, and he'd even stayed with them for a few nights during a particularly brutal spat. Now, it was as if she hardly knew him. Taylor had been with Kam the night of the accident. And even three years later, Connor couldn't look at him without wishing it'd been him.

❖

Connor hadn't spoken to Jake for the first eight hours of their shift, save to ask him for an oxygen mask or some IV tubing. For ten years he'd been her partner. But he was so much more than that. Jake was the brother her parents had never given her. She loved him, and she just couldn't stay mad at him for long. Not when she knew he was right.

"I'm sorry," she mumbled through gritted teeth from the front seat of the rig.

"For what?"

"You know what."

"Oh, that little thing earlier? Don't worry about it, Haus. We're good." He gave her a quick smile, cranked up the radio, and sang loudly to a twangy country song that made Connor's ears twitch.

"Is this my torture? I have to listen to your rendition of Garth what's-his-name singing about losing his dog or his pickup or his redheaded girlfriend?"

Jake laughed and responded by singing even louder and more off-key. He'd known Connor long enough to understand how hard it was for her to utter anything resembling an apology. She knew he also realized he never should have mentioned Kam. But Jake missed her too. He'd known Kam nearly as long as he'd known Connor, although not as well. He and his wife would have them over for dinner on Friday nights, and the four would laugh and drink until two a.m., when Connor would gently put her head on Kam's shoulder and say, "Baby, I'm tired. Let's go to bed." He was the one she came to when they fought, which no one could deny was often. Connor would come onto her shift fuming and red-faced, spitting out obscenities that would make a rap album sound tame.

"You won't believe what Kam did last night," she'd say, pawing furiously through the cabinets in the ambulance while Jake sat on the nearby bench. It didn't matter what the fight was about. Jake always listened, nodding and offering a sympathetic pat on the shoulder, until she was done.

"Why don't you call her," he'd say, and after a few minutes' hesitation, Connor would retreat to the bunks with her cell phone in hand. She always returned smiling. And Jake never pushed her to say more than she wanted. He loved Connor. But he loved Kam too. He loved them together. Kam put a light in Connor's eyes that had gone dark after the accident. She was sharper with Kam—a better paramedic and a better human being. And Jake probably wasn't sure he'd ever see that version of Connor again.

❖

"Medic 884, respond backup to 118 Hawthorne for an echo-four-charlie. That's 118 Hawthorne, echo-four-charlie."

"Hawthorne? That's Dorchester, isn't it?" Connor scooped up the radio in the front of the rig.

"884 to ops. Confirm that's an echo-four-charlie at 118 Hawthorne in Dorchester. Over."

"That's affirmative, 884. All the other units are tied up, and we need you there code 3. Over."

Jake blasted the siren and stepped harder on the gas.

"884 responding. Over."

It took a lot to get Connor's blood pumping these days. Even a routine heart-attack call had begun to feel a little monotonous. But those words did it every time—echo-four-charlie. Shots fired, patients on scene. This was why they were required to wear Kevlar under their polos, even when it felt all but ridiculous to do so. This was when she risked her life. Who needed sex when she had highs like these anyway? As long as Connor had echo-four-charlies to save, she'd never be that lonely.

"Grab the monitor, the cot, and the backboard. I've got the first-in bag," Connor barked to Jake once they'd come to an abrupt stop. "Did you make sure we have IV fluids on board this morning?"

"Hey, relax, will you? This isn't my first rodeo."

Connor flashed him a quick look that sort of resembled an apology and sprinted up the street. Of course they'd done dozens of shootings together, maybe even more. Jake knew what to do. But that didn't stop Connor's pulse from tripping as she reached the police barricade that had been set up around the scene.

She flashed her Boston EMS badge that was pinned to her shirt, and an officer pushed her through. A mob of BFDs in bunker gear was huddled around the victim.

"Haus. Thank fucking God you're here." One of the firefighters who Connor knew well stepped away from the crowd, his young, ruddy face glistening with sweat even in the cold winter air.

"Hey, Ace. What's the story?"

Henry "Ace" Capinelli had been on Kam's engine company and, for reasons Connor couldn't quite decipher, was probably the only BFD she could tolerate on occasion. Ace reminded her of a much-younger Jake, with the same chubby, boyish cheeks and flaming-red hair. He was always kind to her and never overstepped his bounds on scene. If Connor had to pick a firefighter to be on her team, it'd probably be Ace.

"The victim...er...the patient...he's thirty-nine...No, that's not right...He's thirty-four—"

"Spit it out, Ace. People are dying here."

"Sorry. Gunshot wound to the left shoulder. Looks pretty superficial. The cops cleared us right before you got here. They have the shooter in custody already. He's conscious. Doesn't look too bad. But you're the boss." And that was why she liked Ace Capinelli.

"Thanks." Connor slapped him on the back of his enormous six-foot, five-inches frame and tossed her heavy gear bag directly through the crowd. This was her first tactic to clear a group of firefighters away from her scene. Most of them, she found, didn't appreciate being hit with large flying objects.

"What the hell?" one of the BFDs shouted over the commotion, his back still facing Connor.

"Like herding cats…" Connor mumbled.

The angry firefighter, who'd been hit square in the back with Connor's magic flying bag, turned around. She recognized her immediately, and not just because there was only a handful of women on BFD.

"Well, well. Look who it is. The ever-so-cordial paramedic from the cafeteria."

Connor rolled her eyes and pushed past the woman, making sure to try to knock her off balance as she did. But the woman didn't budge. She had a good four inches on Connor, with broad shoulders and big, strong hands that reminded her so much of Kam her heart ached.

"Don't worry. We're here now. You're free to go lift weights or crush beer cans, or whatever it is you do."

"Good thing." The woman removed her helmet and wiped a stray hair away from her face. "I have a six-pack back at the station with my name on it."

"Logan!" a deep voice shouted from outside the crowd. "Engine's leaving! Get your stuff together and let's go!" The woman gave Connor one last playful glance and bolted toward the waiting fire truck.

Connor's pulse quickly leveled when she caught sight of the supposed gun-shot victim. A man in his thirties stood anxiously on the sidewalk, breathing heavily into an oxygen mask and holding his bandaged left shoulder like it might fall off. With one look, she knew he was fine—dramatic, but fine. The engine company had disbanded, off to partake in whatever fraternity rituals they found fit for the afternoon, and only Jake, a few lone police officers, and an ever-dissipating crowd of onlookers remained.

"Sir, my name is Connor. This is my partner, Jake. We're paramedics. Are you hurt anywhere besides your shoulder?"

"I don't know. I don't think so." Jake wheeled the stretcher behind the man and guided him to it.

"Jesus. BFD couldn't even put him on a backboard?" Connor mumbled.

"It's just a superficial wound."

"It's sloppy." Connor snapped on a pair of gloves and carefully cut away the bandage on the man's shoulder. "They're cutting corners, and I'm sick of it."

"Am I going to die?"

She looked at the man, sympathy washing away her frustration. Along with "being the duck," Connor had a talent for compassion. She felt for her patients in a way she knew many other medics didn't.

"You're going to be fine. I just want to look you over here, okay? And then we should probably take you to the hospital so they can make sure we didn't miss anything."

The man nodded resolutely.

"Jake, let's board him anyway. Just in case."

Jake pulled the long, plastic backboard off the stretcher and placed a collar around the man's neck.

"This is just a precaution," Jake told him. "Besides, the hospital gets mad at us if it looks like we haven't done anything."

Connor held his neck steady as they carefully moved him against the backboard. "Let me take a quick look here." She skillfully cut his shirt and scanned his back for more bullet wounds before rolling him over and strapping him down.

"Am I going to die?" the man asked again.

"Not today."

Jake lifted the stretcher into the ambulance, and Connor climbed in.

❖

Logan Curtis was pretty sure she'd never met a more aggravating paramedic in her life. How was it possible that she'd been with BFD for two months and never seen this woman before? Now she'd run into her twice in two days—quite literally run into her, both times, actually. Whatever it was about the feisty brunette with the scowl, it rubbed her the wrong way. For Christ sake, all she'd done was spill a little coffee on her. She'd even offered to go get her something to change into.

She had to admit that until she opened her mouth, Logan had found her kind of attractive. Kind of really attractive. She thought she looked like the kind of girl you might take home to Mom. Not that Logan ever took girls home to her mom, but she liked them to look the part, nonetheless. She shamelessly noticed her long dancer's legs that even uniform pants couldn't hide, and big chocolate eyes that could have been sweet, if they weren't hardened into a glare. But then she spoke, and the girl-next-door guise instantly disappeared. Logan could have just about anyone she wanted. And she often did, too. So why was she letting this one get to her so badly?

The firehouse speakers blasted their warning tone, and Logan immediately snapped out of her funk. She trotted to her bunker gear, stepping into the rubber boots and pulling the suspenders up over her toned shoulders. She was still new, not just to BFD, but to fire in general, and every call made her heart echo in her ears. She wished, just for a second, that she could meet a girl who'd make her blood rush in the same way. But then she thought better of it. Life was easier without love.

❖

Connor tipped back her bottle of beer, took a long drag, and stared at the wall in front of her. She was annoyed. She couldn't stop thinking about the firefighter from the shooting scene earlier that day, and she didn't know why.

"You know that woman today? The BFD?"

"No? What woman?" Jake tossed a dart across the bar, barely hitting the outermost ring.

"She was at the shooting. You know, tall, kind of…" Connor was going to say "hot," because the woman she'd heard called Logan was hot. Connor couldn't deny that she still wanted sex, even when she said she didn't. She was only human, after all. Losing Kam hadn't made her completely immune.

"Kind of what?"

"Never mind. I think her name is Logan."

"Oh, yeah, Logan Curtis. I know her." Jake eyed her curiously. "Why the interest?"

"No interest. I've just never seen her before."

Jakes eyes lit up. "You think she's hot."

*God damn it, Jake, how do you do that?*

"What? No way. Not my type."

Jake let out a skeptical laugh. "Not your type? She could be Kam's older sister."

Connor's heart sank. Logan Curtis did look a little like Kam. Even Connor had to admit that. But the similarities ended there.

"So maybe there's some resemblance."

"Some? The first time I saw her I thought Kam had come back from…" Jake stopped, and Connor was certain he'd seen the familiar pain materialize on her face.

"What's your point, Jake?"

"Nothing. No point."

"That woman is a cocky, self-righteous prick. You know she spilled my coffee on me in the cafeteria yesterday?"

"So she's the 'fucking BFD.'"

"Yeah. That's her. And then, today, she has the nerve to stick around *my* scene and play hero after I told her and her frat brothers to get lost."

Jake chucked another dart, this time missing by several inches.

"Seriously, Haus? You're this bent out of shape about some spilt coffee?"

"It's not just that. It's the principle. That woman is everything I hate about BFD. She just so happens to have tits. She makes us all look bad, really."

"And who's 'us'?"

"You know, women."

"So let me get this straight." Jake took a pull of his beer and sat down beside Connor. "You don't like Logan because she makes women look bad?"

"Well, yeah. That's basically it." Connor knew how ridiculous she sounded. The truth was, she didn't know what it was about Logan that irked her so much. She just knew she couldn't get her out of her head.

It was after midnight when Connor got off the Red Line and hurried the two blocks to her apartment. The air was cold, and the wind shot through her so fiercely she had to stop along the way and cover her face with her hands. As she walked, she wondered why she hadn't moved yet. Maybe she'd go to Florida. She'd spent a week in Miami once and liked it well enough. There were paramedics in Miami. Okay, so she probably wouldn't go to Florida. She'd been in Boston her entire life. Her parents still lived outside the city. Jake lived here. Her life was here, at least what was left of it.

Leaving Boston was unlikely. But she did, occasionally, have to wonder why she didn't leave the apartment. She and Kam had lived there for six years together. The drywall had holes where Kam had tried to hang their first flat-screen TV. The dishtowels had stains from the meals they'd made together. No matter how painful the memories were, they were all Connor had left. Maybe that's why she hadn't moved.

Rusty greeted Connor at the door, where she picked him up and squeezed him against her chest.

"Hey, buddy." Rusty let out a stifled meow but stayed dutifully put in her arms. "At least I have you, right?" He meowed again. "I know. I miss her too." A small, unexpected tear fell onto Rusty's orange coat. "Listen to me. I've become a crazy cat lady. God, Kam, if you could see me now."

Connor made her way to the area of the studio they'd designated as their bedroom and pulled off her uniform, tossing it into the hamper. She picked up a clean T-shirt and stood in front of the mirror for a long time, studying the tattoo on her shoulder blade she so often forgot was there. Two crossed axes in black ink shadowed her skin under the initials K.G.S. and the numbers 11/22/11. As if she could ever forget those initials. As if she could ever forget that day.

She crawled under the covers, cocooned herself in them until she felt vaguely comforted, and allowed herself to cry for the first time in over a year. The loneliness was unbearable. She'd had nights like this before, when the cycle of pain seemed to start all over again, as fresh and raw as if the accident had just happened. Sometimes, it seemed, time wasn't going to heal anything.

Connor cried until she finally fell asleep, trying to remember the feeling of being in Kam's arms.

## CHAPTER THREE

Logan couldn't sleep. She tossed around in bed for hours until she finally gave up and retreated to the living room to flip through the TV channels. It was late. She wasn't sure how late, but the programming available indicated it was some unreasonable hour. An ab-machine infomercial and reruns of *Happy Days* were her only choices, so she clicked back and forth between them, unable to focus on anything except the obnoxious woman from earlier in the day. Logan didn't even know her name, and she was making her crazy—not in the way she liked either.

She picked up her cell phone, scrolling through the contacts and contemplating a hookup. Some no-strings sex usually worked to take her mind off things. She thought of Jill, the night-shift nurse from Boston City she'd met in the trauma room earlier that month. Jill was long and lean, with a killer rack and a filthy bedroom repertoire. And she was always up for seeing Logan. Brittany, the bartender from the place down the street she visited on Saturday nights, was young and vibrant, with a cute little Southern drawl that made Logan's name sound fantastic. She also thought of Sam and Ashley and Liz, and any number of other girls she'd met who'd be more than happy to spend the night with her again. But somehow, none of them sounded appealing.

Discouraged, she went to the kitchen and poured herself two fingers of whiskey into a tumbler.

"What are you doing up?"

"Can't sleep."

Logan's older sister, Annie, was also her roommate. She was a couple of years older than Logan and did a better job than she did at keeping the apartment clean. And Logan liked her company. She'd always been close with Annie. For the most part, her sister stayed out of her business, and she never seemed to mind too much when she brought home the more-than-occasional tryst.

"Well, I can see that. What's bugging you?" Annie poured a tall glass of wine and sat on the sofa beside her.

"Oh, nothing really. It's stupid."

"I want to hear. It can't be that stupid."

"Trust me. It is."

"Come on. When have I ever judged you?"

Logan raised her brow quizzically. "Only most of our lives?"

"I'm your sister. You can tell me."

"Okay." Logan let out a deep breath. "But I'm telling you, it's ridiculous. I met this woman the other day—"

"What kind of woman can keep my sister up until three a.m.?"

Logan grinned at her.

"With her clothes *on*, I mean," Annie said.

"No. No, it's nothing like that. God, no. This one really got under my skin. I don't know why or how. Hell, I don't even know her name. All I know is that she's a paramedic with Boston EMS, and she's the most obnoxious woman I've ever talked to."

Annie let out a laugh. "And this is why you can't sleep?"

"I told you it was stupid."

"So what did this terrible woman do to drive you so crazy?"

"I can't explain it. She's just…I don't know, arrogant and bitchy. You know I accidentally spilled some coffee on her the other day? I offered to get her a change of clothes and everything and was nice as could be. All she did was roll her eyes like I was…like I was nobody."

"I see what's going on here." Annie put her arm around her. "Logan Curtis finally found the one woman on earth who wants nothing to do with her."

"What?" Logan squirmed out of her grip. "That's crazy. I don't *want* to have anything to do with her. She's miserable."

"Listen to me, kiddo. You want to get this girl out of your head, right?" Logan nodded resolutely. "Okay, then do what always gets you to stop thinking about a girl. Go out with her."

"Are you saying that as soon as I go after a girl I lose all interest? That's low. Even for you."

"It's true and you know it. Just ask this mystery woman out, and she'll be out of your mind in no time."

"You're sick."

"I'm right. So is she cute?"

Logan's face warmed. "She's all right…You know, in that long-legged, high-maintenance kind of way."

"Huh. Loge, I don't know what it is about this girl that's got you all messed up. But I do know I haven't seen you like this in a very, very long time. All I'm saying is maybe that's worth looking into."

Logan rolled her eyes and slammed a pillow against Annie's chest. "You're insane. And I'm going to bed. Good night, Annie."

❖

By the time Logan got to the firehouse the next morning, she still hadn't managed to stop thinking about the obnoxious woman from the hospital cafeteria. In fact, the more she tried to stop thinking about her, the more enraged she got, until, as a last-ditch effort, she decided to take Annie's advice. Her sister was right. Logan had the insufferable habit of losing all interest in a woman the second she slept with her.

It'd always been that way. For a while, she'd tried to fight it. But as the years passed, she began to accept that she was just broken. She didn't work like other people did. Whatever part of her brain was supposed to be responsible for falling in love had just never formed. So she'd given up, resigned to a life of meaningless flings and moderate sexual fulfillment. It seemed logical, then, that the only way to get this surly paramedic out of Logan's head would be to win her over.

"You're quiet today." Marty Taylor tossed the basketball at Logan's chest.

"Just thinking. Do you know that paramedic on scene the other day at the shooting?" She dribbled the ball casually and tossed a perfect shot into the air.

"The Dorchester call? I don't know. I stayed on the engine most of the time. I don't like a crowd."

"Oh, please. You love a crowd. As long as you're in the middle of it." Logan retrieved the ball and threw it back at Taylor.

"Shut your mouth, rookie."

"Only a few more weeks and you can't call me that anymore."

"You'll always be a rookie to me, Logan. But I like you anyway. So I want to help you out." Taylor put the ball on the court and sat down on it.

"What do you mean?"

"That paramedic you're asking about. Is she a tall, pretty brunette with a big mouth and a bad attitude?"

Logan laughed. "That sounds like her."

"That's Connor Haus, and she's damaged goods. Take my advice and don't go there."

"What makes you think I wanted to 'go there'?" Logan kicked the ball out from under Taylor, sending him to the ground.

"Please. Just because she's gay doesn't mean I'm blind. Haus is a ten. Maybe more. But trust me, you don't want to bark up that tree."

"Why not?" She bounced the ball a few times against the firehouse wall and then sat down next to Taylor.

"I don't think I should talk about it."

Logan studied Taylor's face for a moment. It had grown uncharacteristically serious and even a little sad, and something told Logan not to push this subject.

"Fair enough."

"I'm sure you'll hear about it eventually. I just don't know if I'm up for the job right now." Taylor got up, crossed the court, and went back into the house without another word.

❖

"Medic 884, respond code three to Franklin Road in front of the CVS for a delta bravo one. Caller reports flames are visible. BFD is already on scene. Over."

Connor's head reeled as she picked up the mic on the station wall.

"884 responding code three."

She hated delta bravo ones almost as much as she loved shootings. She hated everything about motor-vehicle accidents— the smell of fuel, the twisting of the metal frames, the panicked faces of the onlookers. Add fire to the mix, and she was in hell.

"Let's go, Boss." Jake hung his head out the window of the rig and shouted. Connor jumped in, her heart already racing, and they took off toward the chaos.

She could see the smoke before they'd even crossed onto the street.

"You okay?" Jake patted Connor's shoulder as he parked the ambulance.

"Fine." But Connor wasn't fine. She fucking hated car accidents.

"Good. Then get your ass in gear."

They loaded up their equipment and raced to the crumpled cars in front of them. An orange blaze was still raging into the sky, and Connor knew better than to get too close—Kam apparently hadn't, but she did.

"Haus!" Taylor emerged from the wreckage, his face black with soot and dirt, his hair matted over his ears with sweat. "You guys need to stay back until we can put this out."

The police had barricaded the worried crowd, but the scene was getting more dangerous by the second. Thick, black smoke was billowing from what was left of one of the cars, and flames so bright they were almost white shot through the broken windows.

"Is anyone inside?" Jake asked.

Connor had retreated inside herself, staring helplessly at the carnage in front of her. She swore she heard a scream from off in the distance—it sounded like Kam.

"No. The car went up after we got everyone out. Most of them look okay, but one guy's chest is pretty banged up. I think he might have a flail segment. We set up a staging area right over there, by the CVS."

"Good work. Thanks, bud." Jake reached up and patted the giant Taylor on the shoulder, offering him a congenial smile. "That's our cue, Haus." But Connor didn't respond. She still had her eyes fixed on the flames in front of her, her face felt frozen, and her heart was rattling with terror. "Connor. Did you hear me?" Jake took her by the shoulders, forcing Connor to look at him.

"What? Yeah. Flail segment. Got it." After another second's hesitation, she grabbed the head of the stretcher and headed to her patients.

"Are you sure you're okay?"

"I told you I'm fine, Jake. Let it go."

They reached the staging area, where Connor immediately began assessing the victims. With a quick sweep, she noted a teenage girl standing on the grass, talking frantically on her cell phone. She had a small, superficial gash over her left eye, but that seemed to be all. Next to her, sitting on a blanket on the ground, was a twenty-something male, holding his arm delicately against his chest. A small bruise was forming on the edge of his hairline, but other than that, he looked all right too. Finally, her eyes met those of a man in his forties, strapped to a backboard with an oxygen mask over his mouth. His chest was straining to move air in and out, and every breath looked agonizing. But more than anything, he looked afraid. Connor knew better than to ever dismiss the look of fear on a patient. Often times, patients were the first to know when they were about to die.

"You take those two. I've got this one over here." Connor sent Jake to the first two patients and ran to the man on the backboard. Three BFDs were surrounding him, one adjusting the oxygen on the tank next to him, one checking a blood pressure, and the other starting what looked to be two large IV lines.

"Sir, I'm Connor. I'm a paramedic. Can you tell me what hurts?"

The man struggled to speak, his words coming in short, breathy gasps.

"My chest…It's bad…Please help me."

Connor pulled her stethoscope off her neck and placed it to his chest.

"Just try to relax, okay?" She gave him her most compassionate smile, which always came naturally to her when her patients were in peril.

"I can't get his sats over 90, Haus," Ace said, concern painting his voice.

"How many liters do you have him on?"

"Ten."

Connor turned the oxygen tank up higher. "Who started these lines?"

"I did."

She knew that voice. Logan Fucking Curtis.

"How big?"

"An eighteen and a sixteen. I also got a liter bag running wide open in one. But his pressures are holding around 100 systolic."

"I don't know how things are done where you came from, Firefighter Curtis, but here in Boston, EMT B's can't start IVs." Connor shot Logan a look as cold as the January air outside and checked the efficiency of the lines.

"Guess it's a good thing I'm not an EMT B then." She smirked at Connor and fiddled with one of the tubes. "As soon as we extricated him I saw paradoxical movement on the left side. I think he has a flail chest. I made a pillow splint as soon as we got him backboarded, but I think he may have a pneumo."

"Pneumo?" The man gasped. "What's...that? Sounds... bad..." His lips were a deep purple, and his eyes were glassy and far away.

"You'll be okay. We're going to get you to the hospital." Connor patted the man's hand tenderly and then turned quietly back to Logan. "Diminished lung sounds on the left. Let's get him out of here."

Logan got up and ran to Jake, who was splinting the arm of the young man. Several seconds later, they returned with the stretcher.

"Another unit's on the way," Connor called to him. "These other two can wait here. We need to get this guy to the Brigham, like, yesterday. Logan, Ace, can you guys help load? We need to be really careful here." Logan and Ace nodded and lifted the backboard onto 884's stretcher. They wheeled him to the ambulance.

"I want to ride with you," Logan said.

"Absolutely not. No BFDs on board."

"I was first on scene. I pulled him out of the car. I started his lines. I want to make sure he's all right."

Connor finished pushing the stretcher into the back of the rig and got so close to Logan their noses would have touched if Logan hadn't been towering over her. "There are way too many *I*s in that statement, Firefighter Curtis. No BFDs. Period."

Logan stood her ground for a moment, huffed, and stepped away. "Fine. Then I'll follow you."

"Do what you like. We're going." Connor jumped into the back and closed the doors as the sirens wailed into the afternoon.

❖

Logan was still delirious with frustration when she hit the ER thirty seconds behind Princess Haus and her partner. This guy was her patient; she'd done all the hard work. All Haus had done was show up and take all the credit. In a matter of minutes, this infuriating woman had managed to not only steal her patient and kick her out of the rig, but also to insult her rank. Logan had become a paramedic before she was even twenty-two years old. She'd spent nine years working the streets of Chicago before Annie decided she wanted a change and convinced her to move to Boston. She was a damn good medic, too—one of the few on BFD. But fire was where she belonged. Nothing gave her the same high as a building about to collapse on top of her. Still, who was Connor Haus to assume she was just a green Basic? A pompous know-it-all, that's who.

"Jake tried to lose you somewhere along Longwood, but I guess that didn't work." Connor turned from the stretcher she was pushing and gave Logan a nasty glare.

"Takes a lot more than that to get rid of me."

"I'm not one to give up easily," Connor said, unable to hold back a tiny grin.

Logan couldn't help but smile a little, too, as she followed them to the trauma room. Haus was infuriating, no doubt. But there was something else about her—something that made Logan's blood warm a little like it did in the middle of a four-alarm. Haus was sharp, and there was something sort of sexy about that attitude of hers. Watching her take control of the scene out there had impressed and intrigued Logan. She moved to the head of the bed, deciding to go ahead with the plan.

"This is Jim." Connor addressed the group of doctors and nurses who had gathered in the room. "He was involved in a head-on collision with entrapment. Jim was in the driver's seat and looks to have gotten the worst of it. Steering wheel was bent, windshield was spidered, and the vehicle was engulfed by the time we left. Chief complaint is pain in the left lower chest. The area is tender to palpation, with paradoxical movement. It looks flail to us. I splinted it with a pillow, and he's been satting at 90 to 100% O2. Vitals have been stable, but lung sounds are diminished on the left and there's mild tracheal deviation."

Logan flushed a hot red, realizing she'd been staring at Connor during her entire report. Trying to look busy, she began pulling the sheets off the ambulance stretcher and pushed it into the hallway.

"She's good, huh?" Logan fluffed the pillow and helped Jake smooth down the corners of the new sheets on 884's cot.

"Who?"

"Your partner. What's her name? Haus?"

Jake's face brightened with a hint of mischief. "Connor Haus. She's the best there is."

"Hey." Logan looked around and whispered to him. "I know this is kind of weird, but you don't happen to know if she's… seeing anyone, do you?"

"As a matter of fact, I do happen to know. And no, she's basically as single as it gets."

"Thanks. I appreciate it."

Connor emerged from the trauma room.

"I'm just going to go find some…coffee," Jake stammered. "Meet you back at the truck."

Logan and Connor were silent for a long time, looking each other over across the stretcher that sat between them.

"Nice work out there." Logan gave Connor her slickest smile she was sure fell on blind eyes.

"Thanks."

"You really know what you're doing."

Connor looked back up from her run report, her face softening just slightly. "Thanks for your help. You did a great job staying out of my way."

"Do you ever give out a compliment without an accompanying insult?"

Connor laughed in spite of herself. "I try not to make a habit of it."

"Your girlfriend must be very lucky."

"My girlfriend?"

"Yeah. I just don't see anyone as beautiful as you are not having someone to go home to every night."

Heat flooded Connor's chest and face, and she looked shyly at the ground in front of her. "If you followed us all the way out here just to try to get in my pants—"

"Give me a little more credit than that." Logan moved closer to her. "So you're telling me there's no girlfriend, then?"

Connor couldn't help but smile. Outwardly, she wanted to appear disgusted and annoyed with Logan Curtis's cheap come-ons. It was becoming pretty clear that not only was Logan the type of woman who put herself in life-and-death situations for fun, but she was one who broke hearts for fun as well. Just another addition to the list of reasons not to get involved. Not that Connor had considered getting involved with Logan anyway. At least not consciously.

"Not that it's any of your business, Firefighter Curtis, but no. I don't have a girlfriend."

Logan smiled so triumphantly that Connor's heart flipped. This was bad. This was so bad. "How about having dinner with me Friday then?"

"I don't think so."

"Why not?"

"I have plans."

"Saturday, then? Or Sunday, for that matter?"

"You're sounding desperate. You know that, don't you?" Connor grabbed the stretcher and started to push it down the hall, harboring a contented smile.

"Is that a yes?"

"That is definitely not a yes." But Connor found something incredibly endearing and attractive about Logan's perseverance and confidence. Her toned arms and coy smile didn't hurt her case either. Connor had to admit, Logan had done a good job with her patient. She'd correctly diagnosed and treated him, and for whatever reason, she knew how to put in a pretty damn good IV line too. But she quickly dismissed any thought that said Logan was unlike the other BFDs she knew—the thought that she was too much like Kam.

"I'm a medic too, you know." Logan trotted alongside her.

A feeling of surprise made Connor stop for just a moment. "Is that right?"

"Yeah. I ran on a truck for nine years in Chicago before I switched to the fire side. I still practice as a medic here."

"Well." Connor tried hard to pretend she was less than impressed. "That's good for you then."

"I just thought you should know I'm not some cowboy rookie starting rogue lines in your patients."

They reached 884's ambulance, where Jake was sitting in the driver's seat, bouncing up and down obliviously to another country song.

"Good to know."

Jake rolled down the window and smiled at them like a little boy with a secret. "How's everything going with you two?"

"We were just leaving."

"Logan. Call me Logan." She offered Connor one more smooth smile that made her stomach turn over in a way that made her innately uncomfortable.

"Okay then, Logan. See you on scene." And Connor jumped into the passenger seat, no longer able to contain the grin she'd been hiding.

## CHAPTER FOUR

Women didn't usually say no to Logan. Once in a while, she'd accidentally hit on a straight one who'd kindly tell her she was wasting her best pick-up lines, but in general, she rarely struck out. That was why it made her so crazy that Connor Haus had turned her down. She'd said there was no girlfriend, hadn't she? Even her squirrelly little redheaded partner had said so.

So what was the problem? Logan had thought herself attractive enough. Girls seemed to like that she was tall and strong, and laughed in the face of danger. Often enough it just took putting on a set of bunker gear to get them to throw their panties at her. But not Connor. No, this one was different. This one was going to take some work.

Logan sat on the bottom bunk in one of the overnight rooms in the firehouse, going over her conversation with Taylor the day before. He'd called Connor "damaged goods." The woman didn't exactly scream emotionally available, but damaged? Logan wasn't convinced. She needed to hound Taylor until he told her more.

❖

"So." Jake was visibly erupting with excitement as he drove Connor back toward the station for the end of their shift that day.

"So?"

"Tell me everything. What did she say? What did you say?"

"What did who say? And why are you acting like such a little girl?"

But Connor knew exactly what he was talking about. She hadn't been able to shake the feeling of Logan's eyes on her since they left the hospital that afternoon. And it wasn't a feeling she altogether minded.

"Don't play dumb with me. I know everything."

"If you know everything, then why are you asking me?"

"Just tell me!" Jake whined.

"Nothing to tell, old buddy."

"So then I didn't hear her ask you to dinner on Friday night?"

"How did you—"

"I was getting a drink in the kitchen area while you were talking."

"You were spying!" Connor whacked Jake on the arm.

"Was not. I just wanted some Coke, and I just so happened to overhear her ask you out."

"You're such a teenage girl sometimes, you know that?"

"Don't tell my wife. She'll divorce me."

Connor laughed. "I won't. As long as you promise never to bring this up again."

"I can't promise that." Jake turned off the road toward the station. "What did you say?"

"I said I had plans."

"So you didn't say no?" He beamed.

"I think that's a very clear no."

He threw the rig in reverse and backed it into the bay. "No. That's definitely not a no. Trust me. That's an open invitation to try again."

"Absolutely not. I'm not going out with Logan Curtis, so you better get it out of your head right now, Jake."

The ambulance came to a stop, but neither of them moved.

"I think you should, Haus. Seriously. Just think about it."

"Why should I?"

"Because." Jake turned to her and took her hand. "You haven't been the same since Kam. I know you don't think you're lonely, but you are."

"I'm doing fine," Connor snapped.

"No. You aren't doing fine. You work constantly. And you spend all your time with me and that stupid cat."

"Rusty is not stupid." Connor felt her eyes swell with hot, stinging tears. She turned from Jake, trying to hide the onslaught.

"You can't be married to Kam's ghost forever, Connor. Eventually, you're going to have to give someone else a chance." He rubbed her back, reminding Connor that she had to hide from a lot in life but didn't need to hide from him.

"I should get going." She jumped out of the ambulance and took off, wanting to get away from her own thoughts as quickly as she could.

❖

The minute Logan got home that night, her sister Annie was on her. She'd already ordered Chinese from their favorite place down the street and even poured her a glass of Maker's. For years Annie had watched Logan suffer through the trials of coming out in their small Midwestern town. Annie and Logan came from good, church-going folks, never daring to question the values instilled in them from birth. They read the Bible on Friday nights, didn't stay out past nine, and never drank a drop outside of the Holy Sacrament. No wonder being gay nearly killed her.

Logan was seventeen when she told Annie, although Annie had known since her sister was eight and the only girl in her class who had no interest in kissing a boy for the first time. They cried, and Annie swore she'd never let anyone hurt her. Their parents, on the other hand, were furious and told Logan to either leave home or enter a homophobic straight camp designed to cleanse all queers of their supposed sins. Annie couldn't stand seeing Logan spend every day in pain. And when Logan decided to leave town, Annie felt like she'd been given an unspoken choice to make, between the parents who raised her and the sister who needed her. She chose Logan. And she'd never regretted it for a moment.

Chicago seemed like a reasonable place for them to start over together. Then again, anything was better than Blake, Indiana, for a teenage dyke. Logan needed Annie; there was no doubt about that. But what Logan often forgot was how much her sister needed her.

"What's all this for?"

"Just wanted to do something nice for you."

Logan walked into the living room and plopped down on the couch, throwing her boots onto the coffee table.

"Did you get crab Rangoons?"

"Yes. And if you'll take those grimy boots off the table, I'll get you some."

Logan smiled and took her feet down. "I needed this. Thanks, Annie."

"Bad day?"

"You could say that."

Annie returned from the kitchen area holding a plate loaded with wontons and chicken wings and handed it to Logan.

"What happened?"

"You give terrible advice, that's what happened."

Annie sat down on the sofa beside her and began gnawing at her beef teriyaki.

"What did I do?"

"I did what you said and asked her out."

"That paramedic who was giving you the run-around? Dear God, you move fast. At least tell me you got her name first."

"Her name is Connor Haus. And she apparently has no interest in going out with me."

Annie pulled her into a headlock and held her there. "Had to happen sometime, baby sister. Can't win 'em all."

Logan looked crestfallen in a way Annie hadn't seen since they left home. Clearly, this Connor Haus had gotten to her. Annie had watched night after night, year after year, as Logan brought home this girl or that, never really finding whatever she was looking for. Eventually, she seemed to just sort of embrace her status as a stud and gave up on love altogether. Annie hated that. And it killed her to watch Logan waste her time on women who could never give her what she needed. Now, it looked like she'd finally met one who could at least give her a run for her money, if nothing else. She only hoped Logan was half the fighter she knew she was.

❖

Heavy snow fell outside Connor's window as she microwaved a frozen pizza and turned on the television. She couldn't stop replaying Jake's words in her head. Going out with Logan wouldn't take away the pain of losing Kam. Nothing would. So maybe she'd be alone forever? Maybe that was what she wanted. Kam had been special, and not just in the way everyone thinks their first love is special. No, Kam was like no one else Connor had ever met and would ever meet again.

It had been a good two weeks into their EMT course before she'd gotten up enough nerve to actually talk to Kam. Until that point, she'd settled for long, distracting daydreams that nearly threatened her success in the class and, no doubt, a little shameless ogling too. She couldn't help it. She knew Kam's name only from the attendance roster the instructor read daily, but she'd never been so enamored. She spent the entire class trying to figure out the perfect thing to say to the stunning brunette whose back she'd been staring at for hours. Finally, she gave up and settled for asking to borrow a pen.

"You can use this one," Kam said, offering her a smile that made Connor's heart rise into her throat. "It's my favorite."

"I'm Connor" was all she could muster. Looking back, she was pretty sure Kam had spotted the six pens Connor always used for color-coding her notes that sat neatly on her desk.

"Kameron." She smiled again and held out her hand to Connor's, who hoped desperately she wouldn't notice how clammy hers had become.

"Hi. I'm Connor."

"I know," Kam said with the same beautiful smile. "You already said that."

"Right."

"So you seem to be pretty good at this stuff."

Connor blushed furiously. "I'm okay."

"I'm not so good with all this respiratory business. Maybe you could help me out sometime?"

"Yeah. I mean, I guess I could do that."

Rusty invaded Connor's empty lap, interrupting the memory that was warming her from the bitter cold outside. No one had ever made her stomach tumble the way Kam had that first day. However, she had to admit, as much as she hated her for it, Logan Curtis had come frighteningly close.

"I need your help." Logan scanned the firehouse kitchen where Taylor sat drinking hot chocolate and reading an issue of *Maxim*.

"My help? With what?"

She sat down beside him, fiddling nervously with the saltshaker on the table in front of her. "What do I have to do to get Connor Haus to go out with me?"

Taylor's face fell. "I already told you not to go there. You really are a bad listener."

"I know. You said she's damaged goods. What did you mean by that?"

"I told you, I don't want to talk about it."

"You keep saying that. But I can't stay away from her if I don't know why."

"Let it go, Logan." Taylor's voice was sharp with pain.

"Come on. What could have possibly fucked her up so badly? Did some idiot cheat on her or something?"

"You really want to know?"

"Yeah. I really want to know."

Taylor sucked in a deep breath and folded his hands in front of him. "If I tell you, will you back off already?"

"Sure."

"Okay. Come with me then."

Taylor led her down the hallway of the firehouse to a wall of framed photos, where he pointed to an attractive woman in a dress uniform with a small grin on her handsome face.

"Ever notice this wall before?" he asked.

"Yeah, I've seen it." Logan wasn't sure what any of this had to do with Connor. "Who is she?"

"Kameron Shaw. Kam. She was one of us. She worked on this engine, and she was one of my best friends. She was also Haus's girlfriend."

She gave Taylor a perplexed look. "So what happened? Did she win some kind of award or something?"

"She died, Logan. Kam died three years ago."

Logan's heart crashed against her chest, rendering her momentarily speechless.

"What...what happened?"

"An accident." Taylor's eyes glistened with what looked like tears. "We got called to a crash, and when we got there, one of the cars caught fire. The captain said it was too dangerous, that we all needed to stand down. But then there was this woman. She'd been in the car that was burning. And she was screaming and crying that her daughter was still inside. She begged us to get her out, but we all just stood there, watching. It was the worst feeling I've ever had. Kam couldn't take it, I guess. She was never very good at watching people suffer. One minute, she was next to me, watching the car burn, and the next she was gone. The whole thing blew before she could get out."

"Jesus," Logan whispered.

"Yeah. Needless to say, it hasn't been an easy few years for any of us. But especially not for Haus. Those two, they had something. You know what I mean? Haus never moved on. And I don't think she ever will."

All Logan could do was stare at Taylor in disbelief.

"So, that's it. That's what happened. Now will you listen to me and stay away from her? You can find a thousand other cheap lays in Boston. Go after one of them. Just not Haus, okay? She can't get hurt again. I don't think she'd make it."

Logan nodded silently as Taylor turned and walked away.

The snow was still piling up outside the firehouse as Logan sat agonizing over what Taylor had revealed to her. She'd never felt like more of a jerk for trying to sleep with a girl, and that was saying a hell of a lot. Logan knew how hard it was to find someone you actually wanted to spend your life with. She'd given up looking for that a long time ago. But it sounded like Connor had found it with this Kameron. And then, without any warning or foresight, she'd lost it.

"Engine 19, respond to 442 Wakefield Drive for a three-alarm. Four-story building, victims trapped."

Logan sprang from her chair and hurried down the stairs to where her gear was stored. She had jumped into her boots and pants and yanked on her coat long before any of the other guys on the truck had shown up.

"Sounds like a good one," Logan said, giddily.

"Simmer down, rookie. Your green's showing."

Taylor and the rest of the crew followed her, donning their air packs and helmets. They were like a combat unit, ready to go to battle with natural destruction. The engine shot down the icy Boston streets, its windshield wipers doing little to clear the heavy snow falling from the gray sky, while Logan sat crammed between Taylor and one of the other young rookies. They spent a lot of their time as firefighters on medical calls, which Logan didn't mind, considering she'd been a medic for a decade. But she was there for the fire. She was there to wade through falling debris and smoke as thick as blood. She was there to save lives—and not just their bodies, but the things they loved too.

The engine shrieked as they approached the burning building. Three cop cars were parked outside, and angry red flames pushed through shattered windows. The air was black from smoke and ash. Logan's heart jumped.

"Logan, you're on attack with Greer, Fuller, and Michem. Don't fuck this up." The unit lieutenant punched her in the shoulder, but the padding of her heavy coat muffled the hit.

"Sir."

Logan tugged one more time at the straps on her helmet, turned the knobs on her Scott pack, and jogged toward the house.

❖

"Have I mentioned how much I hate fire standbys?" Jake groaned and put his feet up onto the stretcher in 884's truck.

"Not since the last fire, no."

Connor wasn't a huge fan of standbys either. She found it to involve a lot of sitting around and waiting for nothing to happen. But whenever there was a fire, at least one Boston EMS rig was sent to wait on scene, just in case. The medics were there for the people in the building, that was true, but in the vast majority of cases, those people were largely either totally unharmed or dead. Mostly, though, they were there for the firefighters—the fucking BFDs. More often than not, one of those buffoons got himself hurt or stayed inside about four hours too long and needed oxygen therapy and a ride to the hospital.

"I'm so bored." Jake fiddled with his cell phone, only halfway invested in whatever game he was playing.

"You can always clean the truck."

"Don't tempt me. Besides, you and I both know you clean this thing with a toothbrush at the end of every shift."

Connor frowned at him. "Someone has to."

"Some of us have lives to get back to after work, Haus."

She kicked his foot playfully away from the cot and smiled. "A puking baby and hormonal wife aren't my idea of a life."

"It's not so bad, actually." Jake smiled a proud smile only a father could wear, and Connor drifted away.

"Yeah. It probably isn't."

Connor had spent every weekend of every summer with Kam's family in Maine. First thing Saturday morning, before the sun had even thought about showing its face, she and Kam would wander out to the T and take the red line to North Station. Kam always went to the corner store to get coffee while they waited for the train to the coast, ignoring the fatigue from a sixteen-hour shift at the firehouse. By the last weekend of the summer, the small ocean town had grown sleepy and daylight was harder to come by—the last weekend of the last summer. The family had finished their dinner and settled onto the porch for drinking and talking that would undoubtedly last well into the night, and Connor was loading the last of the dishes into the dishwasher.

"Take a walk with me," Kam said, sliding her arms around Connor's waist and kissing her neck. Connor closed her eyes and smiled, still drunk from Kam's touch after so many years. They walked out to the beach, where the dusky sky met the rumbling water. Connor let the waves brush the tops of her feet as they sank into the wet sand.

"You're quiet tonight." She took Kam's hand, winding their fingers together.

"I've been doing a lot of thinking lately—"

"Oh, no. You aren't going to break up with me, are you?" Connor stopped and wrapped her arms around Kam's neck and laughed.

"Not in a million years."

They kept walking until the house was nothing more than a shadow. Aside from a man walking his dog in the distance, they were alone.

"You're acting funny, love. What's going on?"

Kam took her free hand and turned her toward her until they were face-to-face.

"I love you."

"I love you too." Connor kissed her cheek. "But you still aren't answering my question."

"No, listen. Let me get this out. I love you. I've loved you for ten years. Probably even longer than that. Maybe in some other life, I don't know. I never imagined anyone could make me as happy as you have." Kam's eyes sparkled with what looked like tears as she reached into her pocket, pulled out a tiny box, and dropped to one knee.

"Kam, what are you—"

"I always want to make you that happy. Every day. Forever. Connor Haus, will you marry me?"

Connor's vision blurred and her breath caught. "Yes!" She said it over and over again, until she was crying so hard she couldn't, and she threw herself on Kam until they were both rolling in the sand—laughing, crying, kissing. It took them almost an hour to find the ring in the dark, since Kam had managed to drop it. But they didn't mind.

Connor only wished she had Jake's "boring" life to go home to. She wished she still had the future she'd built with Kam.

A rapping on the ambulance door jarred Connor from her memories. Through the fogging glass she could see the BFD lieutenant, his helmet and shoulders brushed with fresh snow.

"We've got a man down. We need you guys," he shouted.

Jake jumped from his seat by the stretcher and threw open the back doors while Connor went for the first-in bag.

"What's going on?"

"One of my hotshot rookies decided to play hero and got herself hurt."

Connor's mind immediately flashed to Logan, although it could have been anyone.

"Where is she?" Jake and Connor jumped out of the truck and followed the stoic firefighter. Out of the burning masses came three figures cloaked in darkness. The one in the middle had her arms draped around her partners, and she was noticeably limping. As they moved closer, Connor could make out the distinctive angles of her chin and her strong brow.

"God damn it, Logan," she mumbled to herself.

Connor ran the rest of the way to meet them, pushing Taylor out of the way and taking his place as Logan's right crutch.

"What happened?"

"Logan thinks she's a big deal," he answered.

"I do not." Logan winced with every step.

"She does. She was on attack, and the lieutenant ordered us all out of there. That structure was about three seconds from collapsing."

Connor cringed and glanced back up at the building, which was now completely engulfed. Her heart jumped as she pictured Logan inside, and she wasn't sure why.

"Genius here decided she'd run back in and get the old lady's photo album. Can you believe that? A fucking photo album."

They took Logan by the arms and lifted her onto the stretcher.

"We've got it from here, Taylor," Connor insisted. Taylor looked as if he might argue but then thought better of it and walked away.

"We have to get this gear off. Jake, get a blood pressure and sat for me?"

Connor went to pull the snaps on Logan's jacket, inadvertently catching her glacier-blue eyes as she did. Logan gave her a pained smile, which she still managed to lace with enough coyness to cause Connor to blush.

"I've got it." Logan finished taking off the bunker gear until she was lying on the stretcher in only a tight, damp T-shirt and a pair of athletic shorts. Connor tried not to notice the curves of her calf muscles or the V shape that trailed down her pelvis where her T-shirt had risen. But she wasn't dead.

"So now that I know about how stupid you were in there, how about telling me what hurts?" Connor shined a light in both of Logan's eyes and watched her pupils constrict to tiny specks.

"My neck, mostly. One of the beams in the ceiling came down and took me with it." She smirked a little.

"Is this funny to you?"

"Well—"

"You're not very bright, are you, Logan?"

Logan looked at her, seeming dumbfounded.

"That's how people get killed, doing ridiculous shit like that. Did you know that?"

But Logan did know that. And she knew that Kam had been one of them.

"So…you don't want me to die, then?" The corners of her mouth curled into a devastating smile that couldn't help but melt a little bit of Connor's briskness.

"Not really, no. It's messy and makes me have to fill out too much paperwork."

Logan placed her hand to her chest and pretended to look hurt.

"Can you put a collar on her?" Connor asked Jake. He moved toward Logan with the neck brace.

"Uh-uh. No way. I'm fine, really. I don't need that."

Connor glared at her. "My rig, my rules."

"You say 'my' an awful lot in that sentence, Paramedic Haus." Logan's eyes twinkled under the fluorescent lights. Connor rolled her eyes and secured the collar around Logan's neck. She couldn't control the slight tremor that had built as she ran her hands over Logan's chest and stomach and legs. Connor wasn't sure why she was so angry at Logan for being reckless. She had no idea why she cared at all.

"You're really lucky."

"Lucky? Or good?"

Connor scoffed.

"So am I okay?" Logan asked.

"Definitely not. But your neck's fine."

Jake snickered a little from the seat next to her.

"You're quick. I like that." Logan smiled at Connor one more time, holding her gaze until she finally smiled back. The quirk of her lips was small, but it was there.

Someone banged on the back doors, the thick, gloved hands pounding the glass.

"Jesus Christ, Taylor, you're going to break the truck." Jake opened the door for him.

"You better get out here, Logan. The lieutenant is all kinds of pissed off."

Logan sat up and began yanking off the collar.

"The lieutenant is just going to have to wait until she gets seen," Connor answered sharply, pushing her back down.

"You said I was fine."

"I said your neck's fine. But you and I both know you need some films to make sure you don't have a fracture."

Taylor, Jake, and Logan all eyed Connor, none of them daring to question her.

"I'll let him know you're going to the hospital. You really fucked up, rookie."

Logan flashed him a sarcastic smile and he shut the doors again.

"Okay, Jake. Let's get out of this shit show."

❖

Galen was at the ER doors by the time Connor and Jake arrived with Logan.

"Oh, you must be loving this," she said.

They wheeled Logan, who was still strapped to the stretcher with the stiff collar around her neck, down the hall to a room.

"Whatever do you mean?" Connor smiled slyly.

"I know how much you love to abuse these guys." Galen looked down at Logan. "I'm sorry. It's not personal. She hates all firefighters equally."

Logan grinned back up at her. "No, I'm pretty sure this is personal."

"You wish," Connor mumbled.

As soon as they reached the exam room, Logan took it upon herself to throw off the straps on the cot and jump to her feet.

"Okay, you guys can go. I'll take good care of her," Galen said.

Jake grabbed the stretcher and took off, but Connor didn't move. She looked at Logan, who, she had to say, was being a good sport about the whole thing, and for a moment she even felt mildly guilty for how she'd treated her. Connor wasn't used to remorse. When she did something, she did it all the way—no regrets, no second thoughts. But something in her softened at the innocent way Logan sat on the hospital bed, her eyes holding no sign of anger.

"I hate to disappoint you, Connor, but I'm going to take this thing off now." Galen unfastened the collar and began feeling around Logan's neck. "It's Logan, right?"

"Yeah. Logan Curtis."

"I'm Galen. Don't mind Connor here. She's just bitter and jaded."

Connor stuck her tongue out at Galen. "That's just not true. Dr. Burgess here will take care of you. And she's much nicer than I am. Try not to get yourself killed, Logan."

She felt Logan's eyes on her as she walked away, a jolt of electricity she'd never expected moving through her.

"Well, that was just plain uncalled for." Jake was waiting for Connor by the ambulance bay, gathering the last of their equipment for the next run.

"What are you talking about?"

"You. Logan. You were downright bitchy."

"I wasn't that bad."

Jake raised his eyebrows at her. "You were horrible. A monster. I'd even go so far as to call you sadistic."

"Okay!" She raised her hand. "I get it. I was kind of a bitch."

"She's nice, Haus. And she may not play on my team, but she's not exactly an eyesore either."

"She's a dangerous egomaniac." Connor loaded the stretcher into the back of the rig and Jake lifted the wheels.

"You know what you need?"

She moved around to the passenger seat and got inside. "No, but I'm sure you're about to tell me."

"You need to get laid."

Connor's face suddenly burned viciously. "Shut up, Jake."

"I mean it. I think it'd ease the stick out of your ass that's been there for the last year or so. It must be getting awfully uncomfortable."

"You're disgusting. And my sex life is none of your business."

He turned the key in the ignition and pulled away from the ER, a slow smile on his face.

"You'd have to actually have a sex life for it to be none of my business."

"And what makes you so sure I don't?"

Jake released a flood of laugher. "Oh, please. I know everything, Haus. I'm your partner."

"I have my share of secrets."

"What you watch on Netflix is not a secret."

"You're a prick, you know that? I've been with people!" Connor said, defensively.

"Oh, yeah? Name them."

"I'm not talking about this with you!"

"If not me, then who? Come on," Jake pleaded, "name one."

Connor paused, debating whether she was willing to delve into this more-than-delicate subject with Jake. But she was never very good at backing down from a challenge.

"Fine. Galen Burgess."

Jake nodded, unimpressed. "That's not a secret. Everyone knows you two were hooking up in the on-call rooms last year."

"They do?!" Connor wasn't exactly a private person, but she wasn't keen on the entire staff at BMC knowing she and Galen had had sex in between calls either.

"They do. But that's not news. News would be finding someone Galen hasn't slept with."

"Yeah, well, it was only a few times. And it didn't mean anything. I was lonely, and she came after me, and well, she's kind of hot. That was it."

They pulled into the parking lot of a Dunkin Donuts on Mass Avenue. "So why not Logan then? She strikes me as the type who'd be up for a little casual fling."

"Seriously?" Connor opened the door and got out.

Jake followed her. "Why not? You said yourself that she's good-looking."

"Yes." She stopped and faced him, daring him to drop it. "I admit she's attractive. But I'm not looking to hook up. I'm not looking for anything, actually. I'm perfectly fine putting all my energy into this job. I don't need sex."

"You're a bad liar, Haus. Everyone needs sex. So maybe you aren't ready to find the next great love of your life. But that doesn't mean you can't have some fun once in a while."

"Jake! I'm not going to sleep with Logan Curtis!" She turned from him and stormed toward the coffee shop.

"We'll see about that," Jake muttered under his breath, smiling to himself.

## Chapter Five

Engine 19's lieutenant showed up at the hospital just as Logan had finished putting her clothes back on.

"Logan." He stood in the doorway, his face stern and red from the cold.

Logan stood at attention.

"Sir. Thank you for coming to see me. I was—"

"Save it, Logan. I don't like cowboys...or cowgirls...or whatever the hell you're trying to be. I've lost good men from stupid shit like you pulled today. You're suspended for two weeks."

"But, sir—"

"This isn't a discussion. No calls for two weeks. Report to my office tomorrow morning, and I'll decide what I'm going to do with you. You're lucky I don't kick you off my engine right now. But you just so happen to be good. Stupid, but good. One more move like that and you're done."

"Yes, sir."

The lieutenant scowled and left the room.

❖

When Connor showed up at the station two days later, the shift supervisor was waiting for her.

"Hey, Connor. I've got a surprise for you. You're going to love it."

"What kind of surprise, Frank?"

"Follow me."

Connor trailed the graying paramedic with the round stomach and soft features. She'd worked under Frank Griffin since she was just a kid. He was a good friend and an even better boss. They walked through the quarters and into the bay, where Jake was sitting on the tail of the open ambulance talking with someone she couldn't quite see.

"Logan, this is Connor Haus. She's your medic."

Logan turned to Connor with an enormous grin. "We've met. Good to see you, Connor."

Frank's eyes darted back and forth between the two women.

"Hello, Logan." Connor's face flashed fire. "What brings you here today? A little friendly torture? Or maybe you're just looking for more ways to kill yourself?"

"Well, this is going to be fun!" Jake patted both of them on the shoulder.

"Trust me. I'm not any happier about this than you are."

"Oh, I doubt that."

Frank stepped between them.

"Logan is with BFD. She's going to be riding with you for a couple of weeks. Her lieutenant is an old college buddy of mine, and he asked if we'd take her on while she's on leave."

"Leave, huh?" Connor smirked.

"Yeah. Leave."

"Logan is a medic. She's fully licensed in Massachusetts, so don't be afraid to put her to work."

Connor winked at Logan. "Don't you worry, Frank. I won't."

The tone rang throughout the building, cutting through the heavy tension that had built between them.

"That's us," Jake said, heading for the driver's seat.

"Why don't you let me drive this time, Jake?"

Connor never drove. She hated trying to maneuver the rig through city traffic. Besides, she liked having the time before calls to get her head together. But this time, she needed to find out what Logan was up to.

"Sure. I'll sit in the back."

Logan rapped him on the back and got into the front seat, and Connor took off.

"Where are we going?" Logan asked, impatiently tapping her fingers on the dash.

"Wait a minute. You guys always get paged first. Then us."

Logan tapped harder, drumming in time with the music Jake had left on from the day before.

"884 respond to 97 Colson Road for a delta charlie echo. Eighteen-year-old male, flu-like symptoms times three weeks."

"They're kidding, aren't they?"

"I wish." Jake popped his head in between the seats. "We get these kinds of calls all the time. Some wuss is sick for a month, and then, at six in the morning, he suddenly decides he needs an ambulance."

"How come we never get calls like this then?"

Connor groaned. "Because you guys don't get sent for the bullshit. BFDs get saved for special occasions, like hauling heavy people upstairs and pissing out fires."

"Has she always been this miserable?" Logan turned and asked Jake.

"Not always, no."

Connor wished for a minute that Logan had known her in her past. She wished she'd known the Connor who had been kind, and approachable, and soft. There were still traces of that person left behind. And she wasn't sure why, but she hoped Logan could see that.

"So how come you're on leave?" Connor steered the rig through a line of cars and hit the sirens.

"I was hurt. Remember?"

She laughed. "I remember. But that's not why you're out. I know how BFD works. Kam was on Engine 19 and—" Connor choked up, unsure why she'd even mentioned Kam to the insufferable woman sitting next to her. "Well, anyway, I know your lieutenant. Sending people to us is his personal form of punishment."

"Who's Kam?" Logan's voice was gentle and inviting, and Connor briefly forgot why she was so set on sealing herself off from nearly everyone who tried to get too close

Jake cleared his throat loudly from the back.

"I said never mind," Connor snapped.

Logan stared silently out the window for a long time.

"I'm sorry," Connor said again. "I didn't mean to be such an ass. It's just…I don't want to talk about it."

"It's okay. Really."

Connor smiled at her, feeling almost remorseful, and Logan seemed to relax.

❖

The day hadn't been all bad. Logan had done a formidable job with Connor's patients and even seemed to know what she was doing. Connor sat in her apartment with a glass of wine and a slice of cold pizza, glancing over the new issue of her favorite pre-hospital journal. Usually, she was able to engorge herself with statistics on trauma and meningitis and strange foreign viruses. But not tonight. She couldn't stop thinking about Jake's insistence that she take someone to bed once in a while.

Jake was loud and often didn't know when to shut his mouth, but he was also often right. It had been a long time since Connor had sought out that kind of companionship. She admittedly missed it—the passion, the connection, the ability to lose herself. She missed being touched. But she hadn't missed it enough to risk her heart again.

She flipped through the pages of the journal, her thoughts slowly drifting to the way Logan's hips moved when she walked and her smile that dripped with sex appeal. She was proud and obnoxious, and no doubt she was every bit the egomaniac Connor had pegged her as, but Logan was also undeniably sexy. Connor shivered with a want she quickly pushed away. Logan was bad news. She knew this all too well.

Rusty let out a rumbling howl and leapt to Connor's side on the couch.

"What do you think, buddy?" she asked him.

Rusty just stared blankly back at her, then pushed his head against her hand.

"I know it's been awhile. And I know she's cute. But it's just not a good idea."

Growing disinterested, Rusty jumped from the couch and went off seeking his food dish.

"Great. I'm asking for love advice from my dead fiancée's cat." She sighed. "Jake's right."

Connor retrieved her cell phone from the end table and scrolled through her contacts until she found the number she was looking for.

"Galen? It's Connor."

"I know who it is. Your name's on my caller ID." Galen's voice was light and easy—exactly what Connor needed.

"I didn't know if you had to delete it to make room for all your other girls."

"You're fresh. Has anyone ever told you that?"

Connor smiled. "A few people."

"To what do I owe this very nice surprise?"

"Are you...busy tonight?" Connor's heart fluttered a little. It had been a long time since she'd made a call like this.

"I'm on until nine, but I think I could clear the rest of the night for you."

"How about I come over?"

"Really? I mean, yes. Of course you can come over. That sounds great."

"Perfect. I'll be there around ten." Connor disconnected the call and smiled.

❖

It was cold and damp as Connor walked up the sidewalk to Galen's beautiful two-bedroom apartment in Brookline. She didn't know what she was up to, exactly, but she glowed with the enticing promise of Galen's company for the night. On the way, she stopped off at a liquor store and picked up a bottle of red wine.

Galen opened the door for her at exactly ten p.m., still wearing her scrubs from her thirty-six hours on call.

"I forget how good you look out of that uniform."

Connor blushed hard as Galen took her coat and hung it on the wall.

"Flattery will get you everywhere tonight." She reached up and kissed Galen's cheek, lingering just long enough to let her hot breath paint her skin.

"Come in. Let's sit down." Galen already had some smooth indy singer on the stereo and a few strategically placed candles lit.

"I brought some wine." Connor handed her the bottle, and Galen retreated to the kitchen for two glasses.

The apartment was big, especially for this part of town, meticulously styled with expensive-looking decor. Galen came from old New England money. Her father was a doctor, and his father was a doctor. They'd all been doctors, and they'd all gone to Harvard. Her father never had a son, although God knew he tried. And when Galen's mother gave him three daughters instead, he allowed Galen to follow in his Ivy League footsteps. Her background probably didn't hurt Galen's confidence.

"This is great. Thank you." She poured two glasses and handed one to Connor.

"Of course."

"I just got home." She took a seat in a big leather armchair. "Do you mind if I take a shower? I'll just be a second." Galen knew exactly what she was doing.

"I don't mind." Connor moved to the chair and slid into her lap, winding her arms around her neck. "As long as you let me come with you."

Galen pulled Connor against her until they were touching in as many places as possible and kissed her until Connor's body was on fire. Connor grabbed Galen's shaggy, blond hair, taking fistfuls of it in her hands and pulling while she kissed her soft, full lips. It had been so long since Connor had felt someone's touch like this, even if it was for only a night. She broke the kiss and climbed off her, clawing eagerly at her scrubs.

"Connor. We don't have to do anything if—"

"I wouldn't be here if this wasn't what I wanted." She pulled Galen's scrub top over her head and kissed across her collarbone and down to the valley between her breasts.

"I just…" Galen's breath was short and ragged. "You never seemed like the kind of girl who wanted this kind of thing."

Connor stopped and took her chin in her hand. "Galen. Do you want me or not?"

Galen nodded eagerly.

"Then shut up." She kissed her again, pulling the string that loosely held her scrub pants.

Galen lifted Connor's thin blouse over her head and ran her lips down her neck. "Come on. Let's go."

❖

As soon as Connor opened her eyes to the unusually bright morning sun, she jumped for her clothes. She couldn't believe she'd spent the night at Galen's. They'd had sex before. Sure, it had been awhile, but it wasn't exactly the first time either. But she never stayed over. Galen was that clichéd player who didn't do sleepovers. She hurried to the living room to find her blouse and bra, the rest of her clothes blazing a trail from the shower down the hall.

"You're up." Galen stood in the doorway in her boxer shorts rubbing the sleep out of her eyes.

"Yeah. Actually, I was just on my way out."

"You, uh…you want me to make some breakfast or something?"

"No, thanks. I should really get going." Connor kissed her quickly.

"You sure? Not even some coffee?"

"Look, Galen. We both know what last night was…and what it wasn't. And I'm fine with that." She smiled.

Galen looked at her, seeming perplexed. "What happened to you?"

Connor wasn't sure. But for some reason, she immediately thought of Logan.

❖

She was late. Logan hated being late. Years of EMS and fire service had taught her an old adage: early is on time and on time is late. And late was unacceptable. Connor was sure to give her hell for this too. The truth was, although she'd never admit it, Logan had been up all night because she couldn't get her new boss out of her head. She'd tossed and turned, thinking about what her next shift would bring and if she'd be able to impress Connor. Then she'd spent the next several hours trying to figure out why she cared about impressing her. One thing was certain—this girl had thrown her for a hell of a loop.

"Logan. Thanks for showing up." Connor didn't even lift her eyes from the spot she was wiping down on the rig.

"I'm really sorry. I was up all night and—"

Connor turned and held up her hand. "I really don't need to know what you were up all night doing."

"It's nothing like that. I was just—"

"Quit while you're ahead, Logan. Quit while you're ahead." Jake came to Logan's side and smiled.

"I don't think I was ever ahead."

"Here." Connor threw Logan a tissue-thin rag. "Get scrubbing."

Logan looked at her quizzically.

"You can start with the wheel wells, and when you're done with them, you can tackle under the armrests. Jake loves to get his french-fry crumbs in there."

She hesitated for a minute, tempted to let out a slew of expletives in Connor's direction. But the way Connor's ass fit into her uniform pants was enough of a distraction to make Logan forget any anger she might have been feeling. Connor looked at her like she was expecting a fight.

"Yes, ma'am." Logan saluted and went to work.

"Are you ever going to give her a break?" Jake whispered to Connor, once they were out of earshot.

"What do you mean?"

"You're being a jerk to her again. I thought you were going to drop that."

"What? I am not. All new recruits have to scrub the rig."

Jake raised his brow at her. "Not the wheel wells. And not with what's basically an old Kleenex. Go over there and say something nice to her."

"Not a chance."

"Don't think you can put one over on me, Haus. I know what this is about."

Connor grabbed a nearby oxygen tank and checked the gauges. "And what might that be?"

"This is about Kam."

Her heart dropped and she turned to him. "You're crazy."

"Am I? Or is it just that Logan reminds you so much of Kam, it kills you to be around her? And the only way for you to deal with the pain is to treat her like garbage."

"Who are you, Freud, all of a sudden? Stick with EMS. You're only slightly better at it than psychoanalysis."

Jake raised his hand to his heart. "Cold. So cold. You hurt me, but I'm right. Can you honestly tell me she doesn't remind you a little of Kam?"

Connor paused. "Okay. A little. But only a little. And that has nothing to do with why I don't like her."

But Connor couldn't help but think Jake might not be so far off.

"All done." Logan approached them and tossed the rag at Jake.

"That was awfully fast. Are you sure you got it all?"

Logan smiled, and Connor felt her legs wobble just slightly. "I'm always fast."

Connor pulled herself together and winked at her. "Oh, I'm sure you are, Logan. I'm sure you are."

Logan's face flashed red, and for the first time since Connor had met her, she had no witty retort or come-on under her belt.

"I uh...not always, no...I mean, only at work...not... never mind." She dropped her head and walked back toward the ambulance, leaving Connor grinning with satisfaction.

# CHAPTER SIX

The morning was quiet, something Logan didn't do well with. She sat in the station bouncing her leg up and down while she half-watched morning talk shows with Jake, Connor, and one of the other crews. The sound of Connor's cell phone ringing caught her attention, and she wondered who was on the other end of that call.

Connor got up and moved quickly to the door before answering, shielding the mouthpiece of the phone as if everyone would hear what she was saying. Logan watched her flirtatious smile and soft giggles—something she found totally out of character for the usually stone-cold Connor—and wished she knew who deserved that kind of attention.

When she squinted hard enough, Logan was just able to make out the name "Galen" coming from Connor's full, pink lips. She searched her memory for anyone she might have met in Boston EMS or BFD by that name but came up short until an image of the charming, sun-kissed young doctor who took care of her neck popped into her mind. *Galen Burgess.* That must have been the woman who was eliciting that cute little grin from Connor. For reasons Logan couldn't really grasp, she was bowled over with jealousy so strong she hated Galen, and she didn't even know her.

"I thought you said she was single."

"Huh?" Jake reluctantly took one eye off the TV show he was engrossed in.

"Connor," Logan whispered. "You said she was as single as it gets."

"She is."

"Then who's she having phone sex with over there in the corner?"

Logan had Jake's full attention now. "What are you talking about?"

"She's on the phone with someone. And she's awfully giddy about it."

"There's no way. I know everything about her. If there was a girl, I'd know."

"Galen Burgess?"

Jake's eyes widened. "Oh, Connor. You moron."

"Are they together?" Logan tried hard to hide her disappointment.

"I highly doubt that. Galen doesn't do relationships. But then again, Connor doesn't do meaningless flings. Unless…"

"Unless what?"

"She slept with her."

"Oh. Well. How do you know?"

"Damn it, Haus. I said to sleep with *someone*, not get your heart broken again." Jake slapped his forehead. "I swear to God that girl is as dense as shit sometimes."

"So she really likes Galen then." Logan's stomach turned at the thought of Connor wrapped up in Galen's sheets.

"I don't know. But I'm going to find out."

Connor thumbed mindlessly through a trauma manual in the front seat of the ambulance while she waited for a call to come in. She hated waiting. Idle hands weren't exactly the devil's plaything to Connor, but they were certainly an invitation to think about things she liked to keep away. Things like Kam. On top of that, she was now forced to try to find ways to avoid Logan while they killed time at the station.

"884 respond code 3 to 1836 Comm Ave for a bravo three eighteen. Fifty-seven-year-old male with chest pain. Over."

"Finally." Connor jumped and grabbed the mic on the dash.

"884 to base, responding code 3 to Comm Ave. Over."

Connor had already stashed her book away and buckled herself in by the time Jake and Logan arrived.

"Let's go before this guy codes, huh?" she teased them.

Jake pulled up five minutes later to a tattered three-family house next to a gas station, and the three of them took the stairs to the second unit with Connor at the head. Inside on the couch sat a man in his fifties, who looked more like his seventies, pale and covered in a glossy sweat. From across the room Connor could already see the restless look in his glazed eyes that usually signaled the close proximity of death, and she rushed to his side.

"My chest really hurts." The man was undressed down to a dirty white tank top, but he looked warm and uncomfortable.

"Has this ever happened before?"

"Two years ago." His breath came short and heavy.

"And what happened then?"

Jake pumped up a blood-pressure cuff on his doughy arm while Logan searched for a vein that might take an IV.

"Triple bypass."

"Pressure is 110/55." Jake began attaching the man to the EKG machine and handed Connor the printout. She studied it ominously and gave it to Logan.

"What do you think, Logan?" Connor already knew the answer, but she wanted to test her new trainee. She had to see if Logan was really as good as she suspected she was...and hoped she wasn't.

Logan's eyes narrowed into focus. "I think it's an MI."

"I'll get the nitro." Jake jumped, the result of many years of being Connor's right-hand man.

"Wait."

Connor and Jake stared at Logan.

"Don't give him the nitro."

Jake scoffed at her. "He's having an MI. Why the hell not?"

"I think it's right-sided."

Connor couldn't help but smile a little.

"If you give him the nitro, we'll tank his pressure and kill him. Get a second EKG and turn up the O2. He needs the cath lab. Probably the OR."

Jake pumped the gas pedal all the way to Boston City, while Connor let Logan take the reins in the back. She had to admit it—she never thought Logan would have caught that one. But she did. Maybe she was sharper than she was giving her credit for. Maybe she had her all wrong.

A team of doctors and nurses ushered the crew into one of the cardiac rooms, where the man was assessed and rushed upstairs to the OR.

"Right-sided. How did you know?" Galen asked Connor once the chaos had settled.

"Logan called it. I had nothing to do with it."

Connor noted the shade of red Logan's cheeks had taken on, and a shy smile materialized on her face.

"Boston Fire, right?"

Logan nodded humbly.

"Nice work. You saved his life."

"Thank you."

Jake, still moping from his earlier blunder, took the stretcher out of the room. Connor followed him.

"You're uh...Galen. Right?" Logan stood awkwardly with her hands in her pockets.

"I am. Logan, is it? You were my neck injury last week."

Subconsciously, Logan rubbed the back of her neck. "Yeah. That's me."

"How are you feeling?"

"Better. Light duty still. You know."

"Glad to hear it." Silence filled in between them. "Is there something I can do for you, Logan?"

"This is going to seem really strange."

"I'm an ER doctor. I can do strange all day long."

"You and Connor, are you two..."

Galen laughed her cocky laugh that probably sent waves of lust through the girls she met. Instead, it left Logan wanting to slap it out of her.

"Depends on what you're asking, I guess. If you know what I mean."

"No." Logan kept her face as still as stone. "I don't know what you mean."

"Listen." Galen leaned against an empty bed in the hallway, hitching her heels together with a suave machismo that made Logan's fists curl. "If you're asking if we're dating, the answer's no. If you're asking if we're having a good time together... Well, a lady doesn't screw and tell." She grinned at her.

*Lady, my ass.*

"Got it. Thanks." Logan turned and left, hating that Connor was able to touch this prick and hating herself even more for caring.

❖

"You sneaky bitch." Jake was standing at the ER entrance waiting for Connor, his arms crossed and his brow set.

"What did I do?!"

"I told you to get laid. Not to get involved with Galen 'Gonorrhea' Burgess."

Connor blushed and jumped into the passenger seat. "I don't know what you're talking about."

"Don't play dumb with me. You're too smart for that. And you're too smart to be sleeping with Galen."

"I didn't sleep with her!"

Jake scowled at her.

"Okay! So I did. I slept with her. So what? I'm a grown-ass woman. I can sleep with whoever I want."

"It's a bad idea."

"And what? Logan is a good idea?"

"Yes, actually. As a matter of fact, she is."

"Oh, really?" Connor fumed. "Because it seems to me like Galen's fun and easy and safe. And Logan's…"

"A risk? Someone who might actually like you? Someone you might actually have real, honest feelings for?"

Connor's mouth fell open. "Well, I—"

"I like Logan. She'd challenge you. She'd treat you well. Besides, she's already into you."

Her heart jumped. "She is not."

"Oh, please. Did you see her face in that trauma room when you praised her for saving that guy? That was more than just flattery. That was her wanting to see you naked."

"You're crazy. She can't stand me."

"Keep telling yourself that, if it makes it easier to stay away from her. But in spite of your best efforts to be the Ice Queen, she likes you."

The back doors popped open and Logan jumped in.

"Sorry. I got caught up talking to Galen."

"Isn't that interesting?" Jake reached over the seat and poked Connor in the ribs, his smile blazing.

"She's nice, huh?" Logan said, her eyes resting on Connor. "She's very nice."

"A girl like that though…she must have a girlfriend."

Connor turned back sharply. "Why? You interested?"

"Me? Nah. Not my type. I prefer leggy paramedics. But that's just me."

A geyser of laughter shot out of Jake.

"Unfortunately for you, I stay far away from egomaniacal firefighters."

"That's not what I've heard."

A chilling silence fell over the rig, and Jake's face contorted as if in physical pain. "Not cool," he whispered.

"Whatever you think you know about me, you're wrong," Connor told Logan. "And if you have even half a brain in that thick skull of yours, you'll find a way to keep your mouth shut for the rest of this little taste of hell we have to share together."

No one spoke for the rest of the ride back to the station.

Logan kept to herself for the rest of the shift, sweeping the garage, washing the station laundry, and torturing herself trying to think of ways to get back in Connor's good graces—not that she was ever really in her good graces to begin with. She felt like an absolute idiot. And she realized this was no longer about trying to score a date with Connor because Annie thought it was a good idea. Somewhere along the line, she'd started caring what Connor thought, and she hated that she'd hurt her by alluding to Kam.

"Hey. We're going for a drink. Want to come along?" Jake was standing in the door with his keys in hand.

"Who's we?"

"Connor and me."

Logan searched the room uncomfortably. They were alone.

"Seriously? Somehow I don't think Connor would be too thrilled with my tagging along."

"What are you talking about?"

"After my verbal power puke today, I'm pretty sure she hates me more than ever."

Jake laughed. "That was nothing. She just get's a little sensitive when people talk about—Oh, never mind."

"But she said if I have half a brain, I should keep my mouth shut for the rest of our time here."

"I believe she referred to it as hell, actually."

"Yeah. That was it."

"Connor's a hothead. She has an inch-long fuse. You can only take half of what she says seriously. Come on. Come out with us. Don't worry about Connor. I promise."

She thought about it for a while. She wasn't exactly looking for Connor to berate her again, or to make her like her any less than she already did. But she also wanted a chance to make things right. If Logan hated one thing, it was failure. So maybe she wouldn't get the chance to show Connor she was a decent human being. She could at least show her she wasn't the scum of the earth.

"Sure, why not."

"We're going down the street to the Rose Bud. Meet us there."

Logan took her time getting changed out of her uniform and into her street clothes. She didn't want to come across like a stalker who was waiting for Connor when she got there. Instead, she slipped into a pair of dark, worn jeans and a wool sweater that hugged her strong chest and arms, and walked the four blocks to the small dive bar. Connor and Jake were already sitting at the counter when she got there, two beers in front of them, tied up in conversation.

"Hey! I didn't think you'd make it!" Jake stood when he spotted her and waved her over. Connor didn't look up from her beer.

"I uh...I hope it's okay."

"Of course it's okay. You're one of us." He slapped her on the shoulder. "Sit down. I'll buy you a drink."

Connor refused to so much as look at Logan, never mind speak to her. And just when Logan had decided she'd probably had enough of the cold shoulder, Jake excused himself to use the bathroom. Logan slid over onto the empty stool next to Connor and thought hard about what she wanted to say. She had to play this just right, and she had a feeling Connor wasn't one to forgive easily.

"Look, I'm really sorry about what I said today."

Connor continued to pull at the label on her bottle of beer and glare at the television that hung on the wall.

"You don't have to say anything. I just want you to know what an ass I was for bringing up Kam. I know it's really none of my business and—"

She jerked her head toward Logan. "What do you know about Kam?"

"Nothing. I don't know anything."

"Bullshit."

"Okay." Logan watched Connor carefully, vulnerability surely painted all over her face, and Connor's anger seemed to lighten. "I know Kam was your partner. And she died. And I know everybody seemed to really, really love her. I also know I'm incredibly sorry that had to happen to you. You didn't deserve it."

"Who told you?" Connor's voice was no longer cunning.

"Marty Taylor."

"Figures. He always did have a big mouth."

"I'm really sorry, Connor. He didn't mean to start trouble. And I definitely didn't mean to do any harm to anyone. Sometimes I think I'm being funny, or smooth, or whatever. And I'm just being a creep."

Connor looked at her for a long time and finally smiled. Just a little, but enough to give Logan some hope again.

"It's okay."

"It is?"

"Yeah. It is."

"I was a total dick."

"Yeah. You were." Connor's smile grew until they were both laughing.

"Let me buy you a drink." Logan waited, sensing the hesitation in Connor's face. This was her shot. If she ever had a chance to be anything to Connor, this was it.

"Suit yourself."

"What are you drinking?"

"An old fashion. No ice."

She smiled at Connor, looking into her quiet, brown eyes that were laden with pain and loneliness, and something in her stomach stirred.

"So you two finally decided to play nice." Jake appeared behind them and put his hands on both of their shoulders.

"Shut up, O'Harrigan."

For two hours they sat and drank and laughed until Jake's cell phone rang from his front pocket.

"That's the wife. I better run before I'm sleeping on the couch." He smiled, tousled Connor's hair, and walked off. "See you both in the morning."

❖

Connor was prepared for a lot of things. She was prepared to shock somebody's heart back to life. She was prepared to put a tube in someone's throat to breathe for them. She was prepared to save lives. But she wasn't prepared to be left alone with Logan. A nearly instantaneous awkwardness swarmed in around them. She thought about leaving. But for some reason, she didn't want to yet.

"Can I buy you another?"

"Getting me drunk won't get me to go home with you."

Logan looked genuinely embarrassed for the first time Connor could remember.

"That wasn't my intention. Really."

Connor actually believed her. And she was unnervingly disappointed.

"We have to work in the morning." But she grinned at Logan as she spoke.

"So what's one more drink? We're adults, right?"

"Well, one of us is."

"Are you always this mean? Or is there a nice girl under that nasty exterior?"

"This is it."

Logan smiled and slowly reached out to push a stray hair out of Connor's face. Maybe it was the whiskey. But Connor didn't pull away.

"Somehow I don't believe that."

She looked at the floor, momentarily fearful that she wasn't quite as immune to Logan's charms as she'd given herself credit for.

"It's true. I'm a frigid, soul-less excuse for a person." Connor smiled playfully.

"I'll be the judge of that."

She couldn't help but notice the subtle red highlights of Logan's black hair that fell in perfectly imperfect strands around her chin. She wanted to touch her. She wanted to feel her smooth skin under her fingers.

"You weren't really going to let me give that guy nitro today, were you?"

Connor laughed. "I told you I was soul-less. But I wouldn't have let you kill my patient. You did a nice job. I was…impressed."

They finished their last drinks and Logan glanced at the clock on the wall. "I better let you go so you can get some sleep."

"What about you? You don't sleep?"

"Honestly? Not much lately."

"Yeah. Me either." Connor stood to put on her coat, unable to shake the tiny piece of her that wished Logan would try to take her home. She managed casual with Galen Burgess. Maybe she could do it with Logan, too.

❖

If sleep had been hard to come by for Connor lately, it was nearly impossible now. She lay on her back, the hum of the radiator wafting through the bedroom, and stared into the darkness. A little drunk, she closed her eyes and imagined Logan's big, surely capable hands on her, stroking up her sides and grabbing her hair. And for a blurry moment, she allowed herself to sink into the fantasy.

Until the fantasy gave way to the image of Kam running toward a chaotic mass of burning metal and gas—a memory she hadn't actually lived herself, but which felt as real to her as any. The warmth that had seeped into her at the thought of Logan's touch shattered into chilling loss. She loved Kam. She would always love Kam. But she couldn't let that fact keep her from feeling ever again.

# Chapter Seven

*Casual. I can do casual.* Connor walked confidently into the station the next morning. For the first time, she was actually looking forward to seeing Logan—or she was at least finally able to admit it. Logan was already inside, using the same tissue-thin rag to scrub every curve and divot of the rig.

"You don't have to do that."

"That's not what you said the other day."

"I was a jerk."

Logan finally looked up, wearing a triumphant smile. "Say that again."

"I was a jerk. I'm sorry."

"Huh. I didn't think you knew how to apologize."

Connor gazed in her direction, heat rising in her. "There's all kinds of things you don't know about me."

Logan grabbed the side of the rig, as if suddenly needing to hold herself steady, leaving Connor satisfied and full of possibility. She was hot, there was no doubt about that. And maybe she wasn't the shallow skirt-chaser Connor had written her off as. Jake was right—no harm in a little fling with a sexy firefighter. Even if she was a fucking BFD.

❖

EMILY SMITH

"You want a ride to the party tonight?" Jake asked, eagerly throwing his things into a backpack.

The day had ended and Connor still hadn't figured out how to get Logan to make a move on her again. It was possible she'd blown her chance, that the Ice Queen had been just a little too cold. If she was going to silence the need to be near Logan, to touch her and be touched by her, she was evidently going to have to pour it on thick.

"Shit. I completely forgot. I don't know if I want to go anyway."

"What's the matter? Plans with the hottie doctor?"

"No. Actually, I just don't feel up to it."

Jake pouted. "Please? You know how Laurie feels about these things. She needs you. And we only do this once a year. Come on."

Before Connor could answer, Logan came around the corner, holding a gym bag and wearing nothing but a thin, white undershirt and her work pants. "You guys going to the First Responder Gala?"

It hadn't even occurred to Connor that Logan would be going. Of course she would be. Every year in late February, BFD, EMS, and the Boston police rented out the top floor of the Prudential building—an attempt to bring all the city's first responders together for a black-tie event that Connor usually hated. But the thought of Logan in a dashing black jacket looking down at her as they danced in front of the Boston skyline sent unfiltered need through her that she hadn't fully expected.

"I am," Jake answered. "But Haus here thinks she's too good for it."

"I'm going."

"Good." Logan smiled, her eyes fixed on Connor. "See you there then." She finally released her gaze and walked out of the station.

"What the hell was that?" Jake laughed in clear surprise.

"What was what?"

"That doe-eyed teenager I just saw ogling Logan. Who was she?"

Connor's mouth went dry. "What?"

"You. You like her!"

"No. I do not."

"What are we? Five? You like her. Just admit it. What's so wrong with that? You afraid people will find out you have a crush on a BFD again?"

"Jake. I don't have a crush on her." But Connor knew that the shade of her face suggested otherwise.

"Sure you don't. See you tonight, Haus." Jake patted her once on the back and walked off.

❖

It had been a long time since Connor had bothered putting on a dress. Lately it seemed that the majority of her wardrobe consisted of brown cargo pants and polos with paramedic emblems on them. Jake and his wife, Laurie, weren't due by until eight, so Connor boiled some rice pilaf, which she ate beside Rusty in front of the TV, and took a long, hot shower. After she was done, she put on more makeup than she'd worn in years and curled her hair into loose waves that twisted down past her shoulders. Then she took her best black cocktail dress out of the back of her closet and put it on, praying it still fit.

And when Connor finally allowed herself to look in the mirror, she wasn't completely unimpressed. She used to care what she looked like. She used to enjoy picking out her clothes and doing her hair. But after Kam died, she just stopped seeing the point. It was easier if people didn't notice her anyway. Of course, people did notice her. Her beauty had always been natural and effortless, and even a messy ponytail and some simple concealer was enough to attract more attention than she wanted—including

Logan's. She'd actually begun to enjoy Logan's attention lately, though. So much so, in fact, that she wanted it back. She wanted more.

Jake rang her buzzer a few minutes past eight, and Connor rushed down the stairs to the waiting cab, trying not to break her ankle in her hardly worn high heels.

"Look at you, Haus. Who'd have known such a girl was under that uniform?" Jake slid over in the bench seat and she climbed in.

"I'm going to ignore that remark because I don't want to start the night out by slapping you. How are you, Laurie?"

The young blonde next to Jake leaned over him to hug Connor. "I'm good. And don't pay any attention to him. You look beautiful."

"So do you. And don't worry. I never pay any attention to him." They laughed together.

"Me either."

"How's the baby?"

"Wonderful. You won't believe how big he is now. He's just this little bulldozer with chubby legs. Nothing's going to be safe. You'll have to come by and see him."

"I will. I promise."

The cab pulled up outside of the massive Prudential building—the tallest point in the city—and the three of them got out. They rode the elevator all the way to the top, where the doors opened on a string quartet and a waiter ready with champagne.

"I always feel so weird at these things," Jake whispered as they walked in.

Connor didn't answer. She was too busy eyeing Logan, who stood with Taylor and a few other BFDs at the bar.

"I'm going to go see…I'm just…I'll be right back."

Jake and Laurie looked at her suspiciously for a second before she took off toward the bar. Logan's back was to her when she approached, but she turned when Connor brushed her shoulder with her hand. Her eyes widened and Connor's heart skipped.

"Wow."

"Who? Me?" Connor said, playfully.

Logan stepped away from Taylor and the others, who'd waved hello to Connor and quickly gone back to their beers.

"I knew you were beautiful...but you've really outdone yourself here."

Connor blushed and looked her over from head to toe, making sure to take her time, burning her gaze into Logan as she did. Logan was covered in black, from her form-hugging jacket down to her pants that outlined her hips and strong legs. Connor's knees trembled just a little.

"You clean up pretty well yourself, Firefighter Curtis." She smiled coyly.

Taylor appeared behind Logan and put his hands on her shoulders. "What's going on over here?"

"Hi, Marty."

"I can't remember the last time you used my name nicely. What's gotten into you, Haus?"

Connor wasn't sure what had gotten into her—just that Logan looked exactly like the fantasy she'd been needing, and she was determined to find a way to make it happen.

Taylor gestured to Logan. "I have to buy the rookie a drink. Do you mind if I steal her from you?"

"Actually, I do. You've had her all night. I'm going to borrow her for a little while."

"All right. Fine. Just remember what I told you, Logan. Damaged goods."

Connor gave Taylor a cold stare and took Logan by the hand out to the open dance floor.

"What are we doing?"

"Dance with me?" Connor asked, smoothing her hand over Logan's chest. She could see Logan swallow hard as she put her arms around Connor's waist. She made Logan nervous, and she liked that fact.

"Why the change of heart, Connor?"

"About what?"

"Me. You've had it in for me from day one."

"I told you, I was a jerk. Believe me when I tell you it wasn't personal. Forgive me?" She circled her arms tighter around Logan's neck until her head was almost under her chin. She could hear Logan's heart echoing in her chest as she did.

"Of course I forgive you. I'm just glad you finally came around to my charms."

Connor lifted her head and smiled. "I wouldn't get too carried away there."

"There's the Connor Haus I know." She returned her smile.

They danced until the mayor stood to give his address, and when they finally pulled apart, Logan kept her hand on the small of Connor's back for quite a while. Connor's body was still warm where they'd touched, and she didn't want Logan to stop. She wanted more. This was becoming a theme. It was becoming a problem.

"What's all this?" Jake asked. Connor was sure he'd spotted her cuddled up in the corner with Logan and couldn't help himself.

"What do you mean?" But truth be told, Connor wasn't sure what "all this" was either. She'd spent weeks loathing Logan, doing everything short of cursing her name. Now, she couldn't wait to get her home.

"I see what's going on here." Jake smirked at them.

"Then why are you asking?" Connor grinned back and took Logan's hand.

"Jacob. Leave Connor alone." Laurie grabbed his arm and looked at Logan. "Hi. I'm Laurie O'Harrigan. This fool's wife."

"Logan Curtis." She shook her hand. "It's nice to meet you. I've had a good time working with your husband the last couple of weeks."

"He's behaving himself all right then?"

"Aside from constantly hounding Connor like a little brother, yeah, he's good." Logan reached up and messed with Jake's hair.

"I'm so outnumbered here. Come on, Laur. Let's go dance. You two have fun." He grinned at them and led Laurie to the dance floor, leaving Connor alone with Logan once again.

She looked at Logan for a long time, trying to figure out what to do next.

"You uh...you want to dance?" Logan asked, awkwardly shifting from one foot to the other.

"Actually," Connor took a step toward her and put a hand on her chest, unsure of what she was doing, only that she was tired of thinking so far ahead, "I'm kind of tired."

"Tired. Right. Uh, me too."

Connor playfully rolled her eyes. Apparently she was being too subtle. "You want to get out of here?"

"As in...together?" Connor could hear the trembling in Logan's voice as she spoke.

"Yes, as in together." Connor laughed and ran her fingers through the back of Logan's thick hair.

Apparently surprised, Logan smiled uncertainly at her and wrapped her arm around Connor's waist. "You know I do."

❖

Connor had found a way to manage her nerves the entire evening. Even being with Logan on the dance floor hadn't produced anything but some pleasant butterflies. But as she unlocked the door to her apartment, with Logan standing so close behind her she could feel her hot breath on her neck and her hands on her hips, she was consumed with a sort of elated fear that left her thrilled and breathless.

"This is the place." She opened the door and flicked on a light. She was almost too high on the lust-enthused ride Logan was taking her on to remember the bunker gear and helmet that still lived on her coat rack. The homage to Kam wasn't exactly an invitation for some passionate, casual sex. But she couldn't keep living in the shadows of her loss.

Logan looked around the room. "It's nice."

Connor moved quickly to the rack and threw her long coat over it, then turned, content that she could tuck Kam's memory away with her helmet for at least the remainder of the evening. She slowly moved toward Logan.

Logan had been with plenty of girls. But not girls like Connor. Not girls who were brilliant and sassy and beautiful in a way that made her think of waking up next to them and making them breakfast and taking long, clichéd walks on the beach. But now, here she was, in her apartment. The last thing she'd ever expected was for Connor to come on to her. She was sure that tiny little ship had sailed the moment they met and Logan spilled coffee all over her. Apparently there was a lot about Connor she still hadn't figured out.

"Let me take this." Connor smiled coyly and slid Logan's jacket over her shoulders. A hard lump rose in Logan's throat. She never got worked up like this. No matter how pretty or experienced, or how rich the women were, Logan kept her cool almost constantly. Not with Connor. Connor terrified her. And she wasn't altogether sure why.

She stood awkwardly near the doorway wondering where her confidence had gone. She thought about running. If she just turned around and left, she could save face and not look like such an adolescent. But then Connor put her arms around her neck and stared at her with a look that told her running was the last thing she wanted to do.

"I had a lot of fun with you tonight," she managed to say.

"I'm not such an ice queen all the time, you know."

"No…you definitely aren't." She placed her shaking hands on Connor's hips and ran them along her smooth curves, up her sides and along the line of her jaw, until Connor began melting into her. When she couldn't wait a second longer, she took a handful of Connor's long, wavy hair in her hand and brought Connor's face to hers.

Connor thought she'd been ready for the lust and passion that would come from kissing Logan. But she hadn't been ready to be knocked over by a freight train of need and want and maybe more than a few pangs of infatuation that left her shaken and unsteady. Galen had been the only woman she'd been with since Kam… and it was nothing like this. This terrified her. Logan terrified her.

But the need won out, and Connor grabbed Logan's face in her hands, pulling her in as close as she could. She kissed her eagerly, tugging at the buttons on Logan's shirt as if she couldn't get to her fast enough. When she finally had it open, she took her time grazing her small, firm breasts with the tips of her fingers and trailing her mouth along the peaks. Her belly tensed and a wave of heat washed over her. All at once she wanted every part of Logan—against her body, in her hands, in her mouth. She forced herself to slow down, the exquisite need nearly crippling her.

"So damn sexy…" She mumbled into Logan's neck, which had grown hot and damp. Logan groaned and pushed up the hem of Connor's dress until she was exploring her thighs and hard stomach. Connor's heart stuttered at Logan's hands on her. Her thighs tightened and she pushed herself against Logan's palm, needing relief like she'd never remembered needing it before. She was already wet. Connor couldn't remember the last time her body had been so wound up, the last time she'd wanted anybody quite so much. She didn't want to remember. All Connor wanted was this moment, right now.

"We should go to the bedroom." Logan was panting.

"That's awfully presumptuous of you."

Logan pulled away abruptly, seeming suddenly embarrassed and aware of being half naked. "Well, I…"

"Relax." Connor kissed her again, this time softly teasing her lips with her tongue. "I was kidding." She took Logan's hand and led her down the hall to her room. For just a moment she thought about what Kam would think—another woman, in their room, in their bed. But she knew what Kam would think. Kam would have killed her if she had some way to know there hadn't been anyone after her—well, besides Galen. And Kam hated Galen. No, Kam wasn't the jealous kind. She'd have wanted nothing more than for Connor to be with someone else, someone she would have liked. Connor was the one with the problem. She pushed the thoughts away and leaned into Logan's arms.

Logan reached out and slid open the zipper on Connor's dress, pulling the straps over her shoulders and following with her lips. Her hands were every bit as knowing as Connor had imagined as they moved over her body with a sort of soft fierceness. Obviously Logan had done this before—too many times, probably. But Connor didn't care. She was tired of thinking about anything but how good Logan's touch felt on her skin.

Once she'd dropped the dress to the ground, Logan picked Connor up effortlessly and put her on the bed, climbing on top of her and kissing her way down her neck and chest, her nipples hardening as they brushed Connor's. Connor tore at Logan's naked back as her tongue danced around her stomach and to her thighs. She nipped gently at her until Connor took Logan's head in her hands and guided it between her legs.

She knew she'd be bad at casual. She always had been. For years she was only with Kam. And then, Galen came along—someone who never deserved her affections but gained them anyway simply by getting her undressed. It shouldn't have been any surprise then that Connor's heart had already gotten just as tangled in the sheets with Logan as her body had.

She'd told herself she wasn't going to sleep with Logan, no matter how much she wanted her. And now she remembered why.

❖

It was tacky to leave a one-night stand without saying good-bye. Connor knew this. But she tried anyway, as she slid out of bed and fumbled for her dress in the dark room.

"That didn't take long."

Startled, she turned to find Logan watching, her naked body covered only in the gray sheets.

"For what?"

"For you to get freaked out and change your mind."

Connor froze, her dress still halfway off.

"Come on. Get that dress off and get back in bed."

Logan pulled back the covers where Connor had been sleeping minutes earlier and smiled warmly at her. She wanted to object. She wanted to slip away while she could still manage whatever it was she was feeling. But Logan's hair was wild, and her lips looked soft, and her skin was bare and perfectly stretched over her immaculate body. And Connor wasn't managing whatever it was she was feeling. It was managing her—managing her and telling her to climb back under the covers and touch Logan, and kiss her, and fall asleep with her again until long after the sun was up.

"I wasn't freaking out."

"Sure you weren't. Besides, where were you planning to go anyway? This is your place."

She really hadn't thought about that.

Connor laughed, Logan circled her arms around her and held her, and she instantly fell into her strength that was all at once tender and vulnerable.

"I was just going out for coffee."

"It's four a.m."

"I'm an early riser."

Logan eyed her doubtfully and stroked her hair.

"You were going to bail. If I hadn't woken up, you'd be halfway to…I don't know…Galen Burgess's house or something…waiting until I left."

Connor shot upright and scoffed. "I was not going to Galen's. And I never took you for the jealous type."

"Me? Jealous? Not likely."

"Are too." Connor collapsed onto Logan's chest and stroked up her belly. Logan was warm and soft and comfortable—all the things she'd never expected. All the things that scared her.

"You're diverting. This freaks you out, doesn't it?"

"What do you mean?"

"This." Logan kissed the top of her head. "Me. Anything besides a quickie with Dr. Good Looks."

"You don't know what you're talking about."

"Don't I? I bet I know you better than you think."

Connor shifted her weight on top of Logan and kissed her way down her neck. Logan shuddered at the touch, a beat of arousal pulsing through her again, and she wasn't sure she could even string another sentence together.

"Is that right?"

"Yes. I'm guessing Galen was the first person you were with after Kam. And I'm also guessing I'm probably the first person after Galen…meaning…"

"You're always assuming things about me."

"I'm right though, aren't I?"

Connor sighed and sat up, pulling her knees to her chest. "Let me ask you something. Last night, when Marty Taylor said damaged goods, he was talking about me, wasn't he?"

"Don't listen to Taylor. He's an idiot."

"No. He's right. You're right. After Kam, Galen was it… until this, I mean."

"And what is this, exactly?" Logan moved beside her and drifted her hand down her back.

"This is me, having fun." Connor kissed her slowly, running her tongue around Logan's bottom lip and biting it gently. "How about you, Logan? Aren't you having fun with me?"

Logan's breath came fast and her hands felt sweaty. "You know I am."

"Good." Connor kissed her again, this time pushing her back down and covering Logan's body with hers. She ran her nails down the space between Logan's breasts, all the way down between her legs, where she changed to soft, teasing touches that made Logan's muscles tighten and twitch.

Connor was never any good at casual. But maybe she could learn. She fell asleep again blanketed in Logan's arms, feeling all at once safe and powerful for the first time in as long as she could remember.

# Chapter Eight

A nnie was waiting by the door when Logan finally came in late that morning. "Where have you been all night?"

"Jeez. Who are you, all of a sudden? Mom? I was out."

Logan walked to the living room and untied the dress shoes she was still wearing from the night before.

"I was worried about you. You didn't call."

"I was busy."

The concern on Annie's face quickly melted with Logan's ear-to-ear grin.

"What's her name?"

"I don't know what you mean."

"Oh, you have to tell me now. I don't think I've seen you ever stay over with one of your floozies before." She sat down beside Logan eagerly.

"Floozy? Hardly. This one's a lady."

"And does said lady have a name?"

Logan grinned again, unable to control the giddiness bubbling out of her. It had been ages since she'd felt this way—if ever.

"Connor."

"No way. That bitchy paramedic who's had you all worked up?"

"That's the one. And she's not bitchy. Just...challenging."

"And you spent the night with her? As in, slept over?"

"As in, yes."

"You stayed in her bed all night long? Without trying to skip out of there or being held against your will?"

Logan laughed. "Yes. I stayed all on my own. It was pretty perfect, actually."

Annie took Logan by the shoulders. "Oh my God. You like her. You really like this girl."

"So?"

"I can't remember the last time you actually liked someone, Loge. You're radiant. Look at that cheesy little smile. You can't even help yourself, can you?"

"Shut up."

"It's true! You've already got it so bad for her. And wait... did you..."

Logan blushed fiercely. "I'm not telling."

"Oh, God. You slept with her, and you still like her. This is... this is groundbreaking. Earth-shattering, really. We need to put out a press release, or a PSA, or something. I don't know. I mean this is just so huge."

"Okay! I get it. Yeah, I like her. A lot. She's just...she's different."

"Hallelujah. I'll make sure to call Mom and Dad right away."

"Oh, stop."

Annie put her arm around Logan and pulled her into her. "I'm really happy for you."

"Thanks, sis."

Annie was right. Logan had never felt quite like this about anyone. Sleeping with Connor had done nothing to get her out of her thoughts. It had only drawn her further into her.

❖

There was no avoiding it. Connor still had one more day left on the truck with Logan, and she was going to have to face her.

The morning after the gala she woke up, for the second time, in a blind panic. Logan's body was curled around hers, and Connor was holding the hand that rested near her face as the late-winter sun flowed in through the bedroom window. She'd been content, peaceful, dreaming through the night like she hadn't done in years. And when she realized whose arms were securely around her, she'd been overwhelmed with fear. Letting Logan in would mean inevitable heartache. She knew all too well what it meant to fall for a cowboy. It meant pain, and loss, and constant agonizing worry. Logan had to go.

After a cup of coffee, Connor said she had some errands to take care of, and that was the end of that. The Ice Queen was back, and Logan was gone. But at least Connor's heart was safe again.

Connor was the first one at the station the next morning. She scrubbed the ambulance from top to bottom, went through all the equipment, restocked supplies, and then she scrubbed the ambulance again.

"You're early today. Even for you." Connor was almost in too deep with thoughts of Logan to notice Jake come in.

"Thought I'd get a head start." She gritted her teeth, bracing herself for the question she knew was coming.

"So how was the other night?"

"Oh, fine. You were there, weren't you?"

"You think you're so slick. Don't think I didn't see you and Logan sneak out of there early. She went home with you, didn't she?"

"I don't have any idea what you mean."

Jake propped his hands on his hips. "That line's getting really old, you know."

"Okay." Connor sighed. "So she went home with me. Happy?"

"Are you kidding?! I'm fucking thrilled. But you look like someone ran over that dumb cat of yours."

"Will you stop calling Rusty dumb? Kam loved him. And now I love him. Don't be a dick."

"Fine. Then tell me why you look so miserable."

Connor put down her rag and sat on the back of the truck. Images of her night with Logan crept into her head—the lines of Logan's body, her hands, her lips. She shuddered with a want she knew wasn't going anywhere, even if she pretended it was.

"I'm not."

"What happened? Did she suck or something? Because someone like Logan's probably been around the block a few times, and I'd be surprised if she wasn't good at—"

"Jake! No. She didn't suck." Connor smiled in spite of herself. "Not at all, actually."

"So you like her!" Jake sprang to his feet. "See. I knew it. I knew she'd be good for you. When are you going to start listening to me anyway?"

"It was just sex."

His face dropped a little. "Just sex?"

"Yes. Just sex. I'm not looking for anything serious right now. Especially not with her. It was a one-time thing, and it's not going to happen again."

"You know, Haus, you're the dumbest smart girl I know."

"Gee, thanks."

"I mean it. Here comes someone who really likes you. She's smart, and tough, and good-looking, and she's probably the one person on earth who can stand up to your bullshit. And what do you do? You blow her off as a one-night stand."

"Morning." The garage fell deadly quiet as Logan approached them.

"Oh...hi..." Connor stuffed her hands in her pockets and looked at the floor. This was going to be harder than she thought.

"I didn't see you after the party the other night, Logan," Jake said.

"Yeah, I uh...went home early. I was tired."

"Connor left early too. How weird is that?"

Connor looked up just long enough to scowl at him.

"Weird. Connor, can I talk to you?"

"I'm pretty busy right now. We have to get ready for the first call."

"It'll just take a minute." Logan nodded toward the door, and Connor followed reluctantly. She wasn't looking forward to convincing Logan she couldn't see her again—not when she couldn't even convince herself.

"What is it?" Connor asked, once they were outside.

"What do you mean, what is it?"

"What did you want to talk about?"

"The other morning. Did I do something wrong? Because I was starting to get the feeling you were pushing me out the door."

So Logan had noticed. And she apparently was less than thrilled about it.

"Look." Connor lowered her voice. "I had a really good time the other night."

"Here comes the 'but'."

"But I don't want to get involved with anyone right now."

"Because of Kam? Is that what this is?"

"What?" Connor balked. "Hardly. This is because, well, if I'm being honest, you aren't my type."

"I seemed to be your type the other night."

"Don't act like you've never had a meaningless fling before, Logan."

The look of anguish that rippled over her face tugged at Connor's heart, and for a weak moment, she didn't want what had happened to be over.

"I have. I just didn't think this was one of them."

Logan turned and walked back toward the station.

"Logan. Wait."

She kept her back turned to Connor. "What?"

"Let's just forget about it, okay? We have one more shift to get through together, and then this'll all be done."

Connor could have kicked herself for being so frigid. Not when she wanted Logan again. Not when she wanted her still. She'd suspected that Logan had gotten her heart involved too. The connection that had followed the heat between them was undeniable. But she hadn't suspected Logan wanted more.

She collapsed against the wall of the building and let the biting cold numb her misery. She couldn't win. If she went after what she wanted, she wouldn't survive. Women like Logan were reckless. They were dangerous and unpredictable. What made them sexy and exciting also made them a recipe for disaster. She wasn't stupid enough to go through that again.

Logan dropped onto the couch next to Jake, who'd been intently watching their conversation through the window. "What's her issue anyway?"

"What'd she do this time?"

"I didn't leave the party early the other night because I was tired."

Jake turned to her and put an arm around the cushion. "You don't say."

"I went back to Connor's. I thought she liked me. I thought we had something good starting. Now she's telling me it was just a one-night thing and I'm not her type."

Jake laughed. "She said that?"

"Can you believe it?"

"She really said you weren't her type?" He was laughing harder now.

"Yeah. Why's that so funny? What? Does she like femmie blondes or something?"

"Hardly. You're her type. Exactly her type, actually. Kam was a lot like you—strong, ruggedly good-looking, a little arrogant."

Logan smiled proudly. "So she isn't into the prom-queen kind then."

"Not at all." Jake grew serious. "I think you're too much her type. She sees you, and she thinks of Kam. She thinks about everything she's lost, and that scares her. But what she doesn't get yet is that you're different from Kam too. I can't explain it, exactly. You're just more balanced. Your soul is different. When I saw you guys together the other night…well, it's been years since I've seen her that happy. Don't underestimate how important that is."

"You're pretty smart, you know that?"

"Finally someone around here who appreciates me!"

They laughed together.

"But really. Don't give up on her. She's stubborn. But she's worth the trouble."

## CHAPTER NINE

Maybe Connor was worth the trouble, although a lot of it accompanied her into Logan's life. Besides, Connor had drawn a pretty hard line earlier in the day. Friends. Not even friends. Temporary coworkers who'd just finished their last excruciating shift together.

Not quite ready to go home and face Annie's newest barrage of questions, Logan stopped off at her usual refuge away from the firehouse—a bar three blocks from her apartment known as the Black Crow. She hadn't been in Boston long before she settled on one of the many seedy-looking pubs that housed the blue-collar thirty-somethings of the city.

"What's it going to be tonight, hotshot?" One of the regular Saturday bartenders, whose name she quickly learned was Sandi, hovered her nearly six-foot frame over the stool Logan occupied and dropped a cocktail napkin in front of her.

"Whatever's on draft."

Sandi waved toward the massive chalkboard behind her littered with complex local beer descriptions.

"Lucky for you we like heroes in this place."

Logan offered her a cordial smile. "Surprise me."

Apparently satisfied, Sandi nodded and walked away.

The Black Crow wasn't a firefighter's bar, where the guys from the various houses hung out and got blitzed after their shifts.

Those places were loud and full of, well, men—not exactly the kind of company Logan was usually after. When Sandi and one of the other bar hands caught Logan in her IAFF T-shirt one night, which she usually kept carefully hidden under her leather jacket, they praised her.

The Black Crow wasn't a firefighter's bar, but Boston was a firefighter's town. And Logan had suddenly gained unsolicited attention and a little bit of hero worship from the regulars. She couldn't say she minded it as much as she thought she would. Especially not when it had brought its fair share of cute brunettes in tight jeans wanting to buy her a drink. Maybe more.

Tonight Logan wasn't altogether sure what she was after. The usual company seemed empty and unfulfilling in the aftermath of her night with Connor. It was just one time. Connor had made that clear. Logan had enjoyed plenty of "just one nights" with other women in the past. So what about Connor felt so damn different?

"Tell me why you're here alone."

A tight-bodied girl with red hair and a soft Southern drawl had sidled up next to her so quietly she just now noticed her.

"What makes you think I'm here alone?"

"Because." The girl took a seat on the stool next to her and smiled. "I've been watching you for half an hour now, and I haven't seen you talk to anyone but that amazon behind the bar."

Logan tipped her beer back and angled her body toward the girl. She was attractive, no doubt, in an heir-to-an-oil-fortune kind of way, with long, fiery hair that spilled over her shoulders and piercing blue eyes that held just a hint of trouble.

"I'm just getting off work."

The girl reached up and gently ran her fingers over the BFD insignia on the sleeve of her polo. "So I see. Firefighter, huh?" She smiled again, the hint of trouble in her eyes igniting to a flashover.

"Yeah." She looked away, still deciding how far she wanted to allow the friendly flirtation to go. On most nights, Logan wouldn't hesitate to take home a stunning out-of-towner who couldn't possibly expect anything the next morning. But she couldn't shake the ache in her chest that had been there since she saw Connor earlier.

"I'm Trish."

"Logan."

"Well, Logan," Trish said, her drawl lengthening with the softening of her voice, "can I buy you another drink?"

Logan looked at her, the need to connect, to feel wanted, coming out as a feral grin.

"I'd like that."

❖

An hour later Trish had downed four shots of whiskey like a champ, and Logan was falling into the soft blanket of several beers and the heavy tension building in her belly. Trish's hand somehow found its way to Logan's thigh as she told her about the ranch she lived on in Dallas and her maniacal Republican parents who finally let her get away from the cows long enough to visit her sister in the North. Instead of going to college, Trish had opted to stay in the security and money of Dallas, and although she was nearly twenty-five, she could have been a teenager still. But something about the way Trish sat so close to Logan that her leg slid between hers, rubbing against Logan's duty pants until her head was foggy, told Logan she wasn't a teenager. Far from it.

"I imagine you get plenty of girls doing what you do… looking like you do," Trish said, her voice thick with need.

"I don't want to talk about other girls right now." Logan ran a finger down her jaw and twisted her hand in Trish's hair, pulling her in and kissing her with a ferocity she hadn't seen coming. She eagerly pushed the tip of her tongue across Trish's full lips, her hands searching for something she couldn't quite find. Trish responded with a low moan, grabbing Logan's hips and pulling her into her until she was grinding her body against Logan's.

Logan finally broke the kiss, still panting and hot. "I live right up the street."

"Then what are we still doing here?"

Without another word, she dropped fifty dollars on the bar, threw her jacket over her shoulder, and led Trish out the door.

❖

Annie, who had grown used to Logan's late-night houseguests, was asleep on the couch, a late-night talk show on low in the background.

"That's my sister," Logan whispered, taking Trish down the hall to her bedroom.

But Trish hardly seemed to notice. She was too busy trying to find places on Logan she hadn't touched yet—a hand in her back pocket, up the front of her polo, in her hair. Logan shut the door and Trish pounced, peeling off her clothes like they were on fire and pinning Logan against the wall. For reasons she hadn't had time to deliberate yet, Logan thought about protesting. She thought about Connor and the way the soft streetlights from outside the window had danced shadows across her perfect body. God, she was beautiful. Trish kissed Logan harder this time, pulling at Logan's belt and then at her pants, until nothing stood between them but Logan's thin briefs, and she pushed the thoughts away. Connor wasn't here. She didn't want her.

Logan let her fingers feather down Trish's pale belly and rest between her legs, and Trish sucked in a ragged breath.

"Fuck me. I need you to fuck me now, Logan."

Logan tightened and pulsed, thoughts and feelings giving way to a primal need that drove her to flip Trish onto her back and ease her fingers inside of her.

"Oh, God, yes. Don't stop. Don't you dare fucking stop."

Logan's heart tripped at the sweet Southern whisper that was suddenly commanding and desperate. She bucked her hips against Trish's thigh as she exploded around her, losing herself in everything that wasn't that moment. She was good at fucking women. She was good at fighting fires. But she wasn't good at falling in love.

❖

"Why do I feel like that wasn't Connor who snuck out of here sometime before sun-up?"

Annie sat on the couch, an oversized mug of coffee in hand, pretending to read the Sunday paper.

"You saw that, huh?"

"I see everything, Loge."

Logan took a seat next to her and let out a bellowing sigh that did little to ease the turmoil inside her. Sometime after they'd fucked, Logan used her usual excuse of Annie being in the other room, put Trish's number that she'd never call in her phone, and walked her to the door. She didn't want Trish to spend the night. She never wanted to spend the night with anyone, except for Connor.

"So? Who was she then?" Annie's voice sounded clipped and irritated.

"Just some girl I met down at the Crow last night."

"You're disgusting, you know that?"

"Thanks."

"I actually thought you'd changed. I thought this Connor might have gotten to you."

The vise around Logan's heart that had been there for days tightened.

"Yeah, well, sorry."

But Connor had gotten to her. She'd gotten so far into her that even sex seemed pointless if Connor wasn't on the other end of it. Annie hadn't been wrong. Logan had changed.

❖

Connor's bed hadn't felt so big in a long time, not since right after Kam died, and for a much better reason than this morning. Rusty howled and jumped on her chest, making sure to let her know it was officially morning and he was officially hungry.

"In a minute, okay?" Connor smoothed the rumpled pillowcase on the pillow beside her, and for the first time in years, she ached for something, someone, other than Kam. Automatically, she burrowed her face in the fabric, picking up on the hints of smoke and musk and leather that were somehow so familiar but so new. It had been several days since Logan had been beside her in her bed, and her scent was still as present as if she'd never left.

Her senses heightened and triggered her pulse, and a surge of arousal caught her off guard. She allowed herself, if just for a single moment, to remember the heat they'd shared that night. Logan's hands seemed to know her—what she wanted, what she needed. But it was more than that too. Logan seemed to know her heart. And the line between who Logan really was and the memory of Kam seemed to blur together again until Connor could no longer pick them apart. But time was bringing these blurry moments into focus more often. What had once been a need to separate herself from reliving the pain of her loss was now evolving into the need to keep herself from losing again. Maybe she was ready to love again. Just not someone as dangerous and risky as Logan Curtis.

The phone rang, and Connor glanced eagerly at the caller ID, realizing she was wishing for Logan's name to come up. It was Jake.

"Laurie wants to know if you want to come over for dinner tonight. It's taco night."

"Thanks, but I was planning on—"

"Microwaving a Hot Pocket and crying to old *Sex and the City* episodes?"

"Ha. Ha. Ha. Okay, fine. I'll come over."

Connor didn't particularly feel like company. But then again, Jake and Laurie weren't company. They were family.

"See you later."

❖

"Tell me what you did, Haus." Jake put down his overstuffed taco and stared ruefully at Connor from across the table.

"I'm surprised it took you this long to ask. You had that eager little puppy-dog look on your face the second I walked in here."

"What are you two bickering about now?" Laurie asked.

"Connor slept with Logan."

"That hottie firefighter from the gala?"

"See," Jake answered, "even Laurie thinks she's hot."

Connor rolled her eyes. "Let it go, Jake."

"I will not. Not until you tell me why you broke her heart."

Laurie took a sip of her wine and leaned toward them intently. "So, wait. You…played this girl?"

"What? No!"

"Yes," Jake retorted.

Connor sighed. She was growing tired of explaining herself to everyone. Why couldn't she just be like everyone else, having meaningless sex and moving on without analyzing every last detail? Because that wasn't her. And her night with Logan was never going to be an exception to that fact.

"This girl, Logan, is awesome. She's smart, and cool, and funny, and Connor clearly admitted she has the hots for her."

"So what's the problem?" Laurie asked eagerly.

Connor looked at Jake, waiting for him to answer. When he didn't, she realized she had no answer. She didn't know what the problem was, exactly.

"I just don't want anything serious."

"Bullshit." Jake slammed his fist on the table for emphasis, the water in his glass sloshing to the edge.

"Jacob! The baby will hear you. Honestly."

"Sorry."

Laurie squeezed his hand. "Listen, Connor. If you're looking for my opinion, and if you aren't just tell me to shut up, I think it's time to move forward."

"That's exactly what I said!" Jake squealed.

"I can't even imagine how hard it's been losing Kam. She was amazing. You two were amazing. But life goes on. It has to."

The compassion in Laurie's eyes soothed Connor's frustration, and somewhere deep inside her, she knew Laurie was right.

"It's not that I don't want to find love again."

"Then what is it?" Jake asked.

"Jake. Seriously. Let her talk, will you?"

Connor laughed tentatively. "It's hard to explain. I know this is what Kam would want. It's what I want. I'm ready. But someone like Logan…" She glided away, lost in the memory of the lines that formed around Logan's eyes when she smiled and the curve of her strong hands.

"Connor?" It was her hand Laurie took this time, comforting her in a way that distantly reminded her of her mother, if her mother had still paid any attention to how she felt.

"Sorry."

"What is it? Is it the sex? Was it bad? Because sometimes when you just don't have that connection…"

"Oh, it definitely wasn't bad." Connor's face grew hot as she momentarily lost herself in her own head again. She didn't want to talk to Jake about this. Or Laurie, either, for that matter. But, if not them, then who? She didn't have anyone else. And maybe talking would bring a little clarity.

"So there was heat…" Laurie was gently teasing her.

"Understatement of the century," Connor mumbled.

"Let me just see if I have this right. Hottie McFirefighter has it bad for you. She's smart, kind, and looks damn good in a tux." She glanced at Jake. "You know, if I swung that way." Jake smiled, giving her a pass. "You took her home and got busy with her. Great sex. And she wants more of it? And you don't?"

Connor dropped her head into her hands, the absurdity of the situation suddenly laid out in front of her.

"No. I do. I mean, of course I want more of it. Who wouldn't?"

"Then go get it." Laurie said it as if it were all so simple. Maybe it was.

"I can't trust her." She spoke the words before she even knew she felt them.

Jake finally defended Logan. "Just because she has a reputation of being this player doesn't mean she is."

"It's not that. Somehow, I think I could get past that."

"What else is it?" Laurie asked, tenderly.

"She's reckless. I've known her for no more than a month or so, and already she's run the wrong way into a burning building and got pegged by a beam. She doesn't listen or care when it's too dangerous. She always has to be a hero. She's..."

"Exactly like Kam?"

Something tugged at Connor's heart. This wasn't news to her. It was something she'd figured out in the hours she'd taken for herself after their night together. What she hadn't expected was the pull of hearing it from someone else. Somehow, that made the words all the more real.

"Well, yeah."

A jarring silence cloaked the table.

"I knew it!" Jake shouted.

"Shut up, Jake!" she and Laurie echoed in stereo, and then laughter replaced the silence.

"Dinner was great. Thank you for having me over, you two."

"You know you're always welcome here." Laurie stood and gathered their plates. Connor followed.

"Let me do that."

"Here." Laurie handed her a tattered dishtowel. "I'll wash, you dry."

"What about this one?" Connor jerked her thumb back at Jake. As if on cue, a loud cry erupted from down the hall. Laurie grinned at Connor.

"That's on you, Daddy," she said.

Jake stood, pretending to mind, and went to tend to their son.

"Now that it's just us…"

Connor ran her rag around the inside of a bowl. "What else do you want to know?"

"Details. Of course!"

"Details?" Connor laughed.

"Yes! I'm eight months postpartum. I've actually *gained* weight since Parker was born. And we've both been so damn tired we haven't been able to have sex in—"

"Okay!" Connor held up her hand. "I get it. What do you want to know?"

Laurie put down the plate she was washing, her eyes bright with curiosity.

"How did it happen? Did she…did you? I mean I saw you two at the party. You looked pretty cozy out there on the dance floor."

"I'm only telling you this because I'm taking pity on you." Connor glanced around the room nervously. "I did it. It was all me."

"You're kidding."

"Dead serious. I was all over her. And then I asked her to come home with me, and she did. I kissed her first. I pretty much called all the shots."

"And it was good?"

Connor's face softened and her thighs tightened at the memory. "Better than good."

"You're holding out on me."

"I'm not! I swear. She's just…" Connor lowered her voice. "Really fucking sexy."

Laurie picked up the plate and fanned herself. "You have to go see her again."

"What? But I already told you I can't."

"I'm not telling you to marry the woman. I'm not even saying fall in love with her. Just enjoy yourself. You've spent the last three years living in the past. Now you're living in a future that may not even happen."

"I can't." Connor took a step back. "I tried that. I tried to do casual with Logan. I just couldn't. I felt things."

"Oh boy." Laurie stopped fanning herself. "This goes way deeper than a great sack session, doesn't it?"

"I'm really scared it does."

"Connor. I know you're afraid to fall for her. I know you're afraid if you do, you'll lose her like you lost Kam. But that's the risk we all take. Every day when I kiss Jacob good-bye and send him out the door to you, I live with the fact that some nut case could open fire on you two for no reason, and that would be that. But I could also walk outside and get hit by the 39. Or drop dead of a heart attack. The point is, we just don't know. You can't protect yourself from possibilities you can't control."

Laurie was right. But Connor would never be able to accept that fact. Not after she'd already lost so much.

"But that doesn't mean we need to run at the gunman or jump in front of the 39. That's what Logan does. That's what Kam did."

Laurie put her hands on her hips and furrowed her brow, a look Connor was sure she'd given Jake a time or two in their marriage.

"But she's not Kam. You have to give her a chance, Connor. As Logan. Not as anyone else's ghost. Not as anyone else's mistakes."

Connor stood with her mouth open, searching for an argument that seemed impossible. Jake swung around the corner with Parker swaddled in a blue knit blanket, wailing and red.

"He asked for Mommy."

"He's eight months old. He doesn't ask for anything yet."

"He did! I swear!" Jake moved toward Laurie and handed the baby to her.

"Sorry." Laurie smiled at Connor. "I guess he's decided it's time for his second dinner."

"No problem. I should probably be going anyway. Early shift tomorrow."

"Early for you since you get there before dawn," Jake teased her.

"I'll see you in the morning. Thanks again for dinner, Laurie."

Connor made it to the kitchen door before Laurie called after her. "Connor. Just think about what I said, okay?"

"I will. Good night."

# CHAPTER TEN

Laurie's words gnawed away at Connor all night, until she finally gave up on the idea of sleep, showered, and headed toward the station. The overnight medic on her truck would be happy to be relieved early, and taking a few extra calls would help pull Connor out of her head.

On her commute into the city, she stopped at a cafe she knew served coffee strong enough to put hair on her knuckles and ordered a large with cream and a bagel. Aside from the lone barista behind the pastry counter, the place was empty, lit only by a flickering overhead and the display case. In spite of the busy Alston neighborhood, the streets were barren, save for a few waiting cabs and an idling public bus. In an hour or so, the city would wake up, and, even in early March, the streets would be littered with students and pedestrians and bicyclists. This was Connor's favorite time of day.

The barista handed her the coffee and she took a long, soothing sip, not bothering to turn around when the chimes on the front door jangled. It wasn't unusual for other patrons to find their way into the cafe this time of morning. Even at such an ungodly hour, a few scattered businessmen and construction workers would wander in, puffy-eyed and grumpy, and mutter for something to get them through the day.

"Kind of early to start your shift, isn't it?"

Connor didn't have to turn around to recognize what had become a familiar quickening of her pulse at the smooth, smoky voice and musky smell. But she did anyway. "Yeah, well, I couldn't sleep."

Logan stood in front of her, the shadows under her eyes letting Connor know she probably hadn't been doing much sleeping either. Connor wondered what had been keeping her up. Or, rather, who had been keeping her up. Then she quickly reminded herself she wasn't supposed to care. "Sorry to hear that."

Logan stepped away from her and ordered her coffee, her words short and angry. "So, what? You've taken to stalking me now?" She poured copious amounts of sugar in the cup, not bothering to look at Connor. "This is my neighborhood, actually."

Connor looked her over from head to toe, noting the hooded sweatshirt and running shoes that accompanied a cool gleam of sweat on her forehead. "You always get up this early?"

"Yeah." Logan fanned the steam away from her coffee and took a sip. Connor had insisted she wanted nothing to do with Logan, but she couldn't help her barrage of questions. "I run every morning before my shift."

"I didn't know you were an early riser."

"I guess there's a lot you don't know about me," Logan grumbled and headed toward the door.

"Logan." Connor wasn't sure why she'd called her back. Just that she didn't want her to leave. Not like this, at least. She hated the clipped tone in her usually kind and generous voice. She hated how little Logan seemed to notice her now.

"Yeah?"

"Maybe I'll see you on scene today."

"Maybe." Logan turned again, her hand on the door handle, before she spun around. "Listen. Do you want to go somewhere with me?"

Connor's initial surprise gave way to a small grin at Logan's softening.

"Like, now?"

"Yes, now. Relax. It's not a date or anything like that. I know your shift doesn't start for another couple of hours, and I thought you might want to see this."

Connor hesitated, then picked up her coffee and took a step toward Logan. They only had a couple of hours. How much harm could she possibly do?

"Sure. Why not?"

They walked out of the cafe and down the still-dim street where the early spring sun was struggling to rise. A few more cars had taken to the road, and a lone train passed across what was usually a busy intersection.

"Are you always out here this time of day?" Connor asked.

"Every morning."

"You know it's kind of dangerous here, right?"

Logan laughed. "I was Chicago EMS for ten years. This little neighborhood can't handle me."

"Has anyone ever told you you're arrogant?"

"A few people, yes." Logan grinned fiercely, and Connor's breath caught in her throat as the dusky light sketched the angular lines of her jaw and the wild strands of her hair.

"Well then, did they tell you that's hardly an attractive quality?" Connor jammed her hand in her pocket as she walked, suddenly afraid if she didn't, she would no longer be able to control the urge to reach out and touch her.

"I don't think I'm arrogant. Just misunderstood."

"That's what all the players say about themselves."

"Is that what you think of me? That I'm a player?" Logan led her down a dark alley and into the neighborhood park.

"I've heard a thing or two about you. Guys talk."

"You don't really believe everything you hear, do you?"

"Only when it's probably true."

"Come on." Logan reached behind her and took Connor's hand, running her thumb over the top. "We're almost there."

They walked until they reached a rickety bench in the middle of the park.

"There." Logan pointed up through a clearing of trees. The Boston skyline stood bold and powerful as the sun rose behind it with trails of pink and orange. The lights of the buildings were a dull contrast to the morning.

Connor sat down. "It's beautiful."

"I know. I found it one morning when I was running. Right after we moved here."

Logan sat down beside her and they watched the sky lighten, bright beams of color rolling over the skyscrapers and washing the city in what could only feel like the promise of hope. A new day. Somehow, watching the sun come up over the city gave Connor that.

Neither of them spoke another word. Almost unconsciously, she inched her hand toward Logan's and took it in hers, winding her smaller, thin fingers through Logan's callused ones. She couldn't help but notice how perfectly, how naturally, they fit together. She didn't want to think about it. She just wanted to feel her there, to enjoy the fleeting moments of peace and joy before she shattered them out of fear.

Going to the park with Logan had been a colossal mistake. After they finished their coffees and talking about their families and their jobs and their pasts, Connor finally glanced at her watch. The sun was already long since up, and somehow, she was late for her shift. She'd never been late for one. She ran the five blocks to the station, her chest heaving as she threw open the bay door.

"What the hell happened to you?" Jake asked.

"Everything okay? Did I miss a call?"

"You're fine. Take a load off. I covered for you with the captain."

Connor exhaled and sat on the back of the rig. "Good."

"Overslept?"

"Hardly. I was up before the sun was even...Never mind." Connor didn't want to explain to Jake where she'd been or who she'd been with.

"So then what..." Jake's eyes brightened. "You were with her, weren't you?!"

No point in lying. Jake always had a way of getting to the bottom of everything anyway. Besides, Connor was tired. She didn't want to lie to him anymore than she wanted to lie to herself.

"Yeah. I ran into her at Pavement when I was getting coffee." Connor flushed when she remembered the way Logan looked in her running shorts that showed off her hard, muscled legs.

"That's it?"

"Then she took me to the park by the university and showed me this great spot that overlooks the whole city."

"The big bad player has a romantic side, huh?"

Connor smiled. It was romantic, but not because of the view or the time of day. Logan hadn't planned any of it. And Connor bet she was one of the few to have shared that with her.

Jake continued to stare at her, obviously waiting. "And then what?"

"What do you mean, 'and then what'?"

"You're twenty minutes late, which for you might as well be twenty hours late, and all you can tell me is that you were sitting on a park bench somewhere watching the sun rise?"

"Pretty much." Connor stood up and Jake chased her.

"Are you going out with her now? Did you at least kiss her? Come on. You're such a prude!"

The overhead tone drowned out the rest of Jake's pleas, and Connor turned to him with a satisfied smirk. She put her hand dramatically to her ear. "What's that? Sorry, Jake. I can't hear you. We've got a call. Let's go."

She jumped into the passenger seat of the truck and Jake followed, grumbling.

"Medic 884 respond to 49 Coulter Street for a bravo nine nine. Forty-three-year-old male, possible overdose. Over."

Jake had already pulled out of the station by the time Connor picked up the mic.

"884 responding to 49 Coulter Street. Over."

"884, be advised no PD on scene. We have an officer on his way, and right now the patient is under control, but if the scene escalates, get out of there. Over."

"Copy that. We'll be fine. Over."

Jake pulled up outside an old building with weather-beaten shutters falling off the windows and yellowing paint chipping away from the siding. They knew this neighborhood. It was notoriously bad, with reports of drug deals gone wrong nearly every month. Connor thought about what Jake's wife, Laurie, had said to her at dinner the other night—*some nut job could open fire on you two and that'd be that.* Maybe she had a point.

Connor's job wasn't exactly free of danger either. It wasn't like she worked in an accounting office. She wore a Kevlar vest to work every day. And here she was judging Logan for running into burning buildings at a moment's notice. No. It was hardly the same thing. Connor didn't chase death as some kind of badge of honor. She only tried to keep people from it.

"Guess who's here already," Jake said, pointing to the number on the BFD engine parked along the street. Logan's engine. Of course.

"Don't you dare cause trouble, Jacob O'Harrigan. I will not hesitate to call your wife."

She glared at him once more and jumped out of the truck to get the stretcher. Logan and Taylor were in the living room when they entered the small apartment. The floor was covered in old magazines and empty take-out wrappers, and a few used needles were scattered about.

"Watch it," Logan said. "There're sharps everywhere. This place is a disaster."

Connor and Jake tiptoed over the minefield and made their way toward a battered recliner where a man in his forties, looking more like his sixties, sat despondently. He was tall and thin, with sharp features and a tuft of salt-and-pepper hair that poked out from under a Red Sox cap. His gaze was fixed straight ahead and his breath was shallow and raspy.

"Get a name?" Connor asked.

"No. But I found an empty bag of what was probably heroin at some point on the table over there."

Connor grabbed the man's wrist and felt for a pulse. It was slow and weak, but it was there.

"Jake, I want to give this guy some Narcan."

Logan eyed her anxiously. "Here? Are you sure?"

"His respirations are slow. Pupils are tiny. If we don't give it to him now he could arrest on us."

"Better than waking up and puking on us."

"Jake. The Narcan. Now."

Jake reached into the med box and put together a syringe full of the drug intended to reverse the effects of an opioid like heroin. Unfortunately, the drug often worked too well, and the patient would be ripped from their high into an often-nauseous rage. Connor approached the man and carefully injected the Narcan into his bicep as Logan took a protective step closer to her.

"Aww, man, what the fuck?!" As if struck by a bolt of lightning, the man shot up out of his chair and charged them.

"Shit." Connor tried to be the best duck she could be—cool on the surface. But her heart was fluttering and she wanted to run. Jake hit the ground, nearly army-crawling out of the room. No one saw the handgun that had been stuck in the waistband of the man's jeans.

"Gun. Gun." Logan said, her always-steady voice barely wavering under the tension of the moment. "Get down."

Connor watched her from the corner of her eye, grateful for Logan's strength and control. She thought about losing Logan, and the world suddenly grew a little darker.

"Connor, get down!"

The man slowly lifted the gun and angled it toward them, first at Taylor, and then at Connor, until the tip was just inches from her nose. *This is it. This is how I die.*

"I'll kill all you fuckers. You hear me? You come into my house and take my dope, I'll kill you all."

Connor was so still she was hardly breathing.

"Just put down the gun, sir, and we'll leave," Logan said in a rational tone. She moved closer to Connor, her hands up over her head. When the man didn't budge, Connor knew Logan would act. It was too much for her to sit by and watch people get hurt. In one swift movement, she lunged at him, wrapped her hand around the barrel of the gun, and wrestled it away from Connor's head. For what felt like several agonizing minutes, Logan forced the thinner man's arm down while Taylor wrapped his tree-trunk arms around him from behind. A shot fired, ricocheting off the floor and through the wall, and Jake continued his army crawl all the way out the front door. Connor closed her eyes at the blast, sure that Logan was about to succumb to her need to be a hero. This was exactly what she'd always known about Logan. And now they were both going to die.

When she opened her eyes again, Taylor and Logan had the man pinned to the ground, his arms up behind his head and the gun safely under Logan's boot. Connor's heart soared at the sight of Logan, unharmed. She was foolish and crazy and nearly got herself killed. But she'd also saved her life.

As if on cue, a lone police officer burst through the front door, gun raised, shouting, "Everybody on the ground!"

"Thanks for the backup," Taylor said with a grin. "How about some handcuffs?"

"What the—"

"Guess he didn't like the Narcan you gave him," Logan said, her eyes locked on Connor. For a moment, it was just the two of them, connected, real…alive.

"Everyone okay?"

"We're fine," Connor added. "Just get him out of here."

The officer tightened the cuffs around the man's bony wrists, and Taylor and Logan released him just as Jake appeared from around the corner, pale and sickly looking.

"You guys are alive?!" he squeaked.

Connor moved toward him and put her arm around him. "No thanks to you."

"Hey, scene safety first!"

She smiled at him, more grateful than ever to have a friend like Jake in her life. "Go take the stretcher out to the truck, will you?"

"Gladly."

Taylor followed him outside, and Connor was alone with Logan.

For a long time, Connor just stared at her, a growing storm of fury building until Logan took a step back. And then she walked toward her, determined and angry, and slammed her hands against Logan's chest, shoving her back toward the wall.

"Are you out of your damn mind?" she yelled, pushing her again for emphasis.

Logan didn't answer but instead grinned back wryly at her.

"You just took down a gunman…unarmed!" Connor was screaming so loudly now her voice quivered, and hot, salty tears built up behind the rage until she was sobbing. Then her anger gave way to gratitude as she collapsed against Logan.

"You could have gotten yourself killed."

"Hey." Logan pulled her close, wrapping her in her arms until they could both feel safe again. Connor was warm, and happy, and felt like the sunrise over the skyline that morning. "I didn't. I'm okay," Logan said. "We're both okay."

Connor never let anyone see her cry. But she didn't care. All she cared about was Logan, safe, her arms around her.

"I'm sorry I was reckless. I just couldn't live with anything hurting you." Logan lifted her chin in her hand and wiped a tear away.

"How did you learn to do that anyway?"

"My brother's a cop. He insisted if I was going to be a medic, I had to learn how to defend myself."

Connor's crying slowed and her breath leveled, a steady smile replacing the fear. "Has anyone ever told you you're an idiot?"

"A few people." Logan smiled back at her.

"You saved my life."

Logan folded her in her arms again and the tears threatened to return. She noticed Logan's eyes growing glassy now too. As Logan buried her face in Connor's neck, Connor wondered just how much of her heroism had to do with who she was, and how much of it had to do with who Connor was becoming to her.

"What are you doing tonight?"

Connor looked up at her, the familiar feelings of skepticism resurfacing.

"Why?"

"Have dinner with me," Logan asked.

"I thought we already went over this."

"Just as friends. Coworkers. Whatever. We almost died today. I think we owe it to ourselves to celebrate a little, right?"

Heat pulsed through Connor's body as Logan smiled her cool smile that no doubt made a million girls feel like they were the only one. She'd already decided against letting Logan in. The idea wasn't any better in the wake of near death than it was before. Then again…it was just dinner.

"Come on. We both get off at seven, right? And we both have to eat, don't we? Besides, I did save your life today."

Connor punched her lightly on the shoulder and scowled. "Okay, fine. But only because we both have to eat. Right?"

Logan beamed. "I'll swing by the station at seven thirty and pick you up."

"Fine." Connor got up and walked out of the house, the excitement she'd been unwilling to accept bubbling to the surface.

Jake messed with her from the driver's seat. "What took so long?"

"Just clearing up some plans." She smiled again, turning from Jake in hopes of avoiding any more interrogation.

"Plans with Logan?"

"Mmmm. I'll never tell."

"You have to. Please, Connor. Laur's been asking me for updates every day. She's going crazy at home with Parker. You've got to give her something to work with!"

Connor chuckled. "So I need to tell you the details of my personal life for Laurie?"

"Yes. Just for Laurie. I couldn't care less about all this girl-talk business."

"Right. Well, you can go ahead and tell your wife that I'm having dinner with Logan after work tonight."

Jake nearly bounced out of his seat. "A date?!"

"Not a date. Just a thank-you. A celebration of not dying today."

"Right. Well, call it what you want to, Haus. But it's a date."

"Fine. Then maybe it's a date." Somehow, this time the idea wasn't so frightening.

# CHAPTER ELEVEN

The rest of the day had been quiet, at least on the surface. But Connor's head was spinning with thoughts of seeing Logan. At seven on the dot, she checked to make sure the rig was stocked for tomorrow and went to her locker to retrieve her street clothes. Making use of the tiny station shower, she got ready as best she could, wondering why she cared quite so much how she looked all of a sudden.

Jake poked his head through the bathroom door, where Connor was busy fussing with her hair. "I think your date's here."

"What?"

"In the bay."

Connor dismissed him, her pulse hammering in her ears. Satisfied that her hair looked as good as it ever would, she left the bathroom and went in search of Logan. She found her in the garage, leaning against the side of the ambulance. Her arms were crossed casually, and she wore black jeans with black boots and a weathered leather jacket that outlined her shoulders and chest as well as it did her dangerous spirit. Confidence and sex wafted off of her like a sea breeze, and Connor's legs shook. Her mind blanked. No way was this going to just be dinner.

"Hi." Connor smiled shyly at the ground and moved toward her, feeling like the exuberant adolescent she thought had died with Kam.

"You ready to go?"

"All set."

Logan held out her arm and Connor took it, enthralled by the contrast of the bad boy and the gentleman. This woman really did have it all going for her. She probably knew it too.

"Let me guess. You have a motorcycle waiting for me out there, don't you?"

"No." Logan laughed. "That shit's dangerous."

They walked out to the street where a cabbie waited, tapping his fingers on the dash and glancing at the meter. A cab was the last thing she'd expected from Logan. She had to laugh at herself for making so many assumptions about her. It wasn't fair when most of what she knew about Logan was based on her own theories.

"158 Russell," Logan told him after she'd opened the door and let Connor in. It was a bit odd to give an address instead of the name of a restaurant, but Connor didn't think much of it. Instead, she opted for enjoying the feel of Logan's body pressed against hers—her shoulder against her shoulder, her leg against her leg.

They were already a few blocks away before she asked, "Where are you taking me, anyway?"

"Best place in town." Logan smiled at her, and Connor found herself having to fight to think. It didn't really matter where they were going. A few minutes later, the cab came to a stop on a residential street lined with old Victorians.

"Funny. 'Best place in town' looks an awful lot like somewhere you may or may not live," Connor said. Logan returned a smile, handed the cabbie a wrinkled twenty-dollar bill, and came around to open the door for Connor.

"Would you believe me if I said I wasn't trying to get in your pants?"

"Not for a second." But Connor hadn't fully convinced herself yet that wasn't what she wanted again. Not when Logan's ass looked so painfully good in her tight jeans. Not when her body still burned where Logan had touched her.

Logan led Connor up a set of stone steps and into the old house.

"Really. What are you up to?" Connor asked, skeptical of the situation. "I thought we were just going to dinner."

"We are." Logan unlocked a door on the ground floor and ushered Connor inside.

"You aren't trying to tell me you can actually cook."

"Why are you always so quick to judge? Of course I can cook." Logan took Connor's coat and draped it over a kitchen chair. "Wine? Beer?"

"Beer. If you have it."

Logan went right to work shuffling around the oversized kitchen, popping the tops off two bottles of imported beer and pulling out fresh herbs and steak and garlic from what was clearly a well-stocked refrigerator while Connor searched the room, trying to piece together the puzzle that was Logan's life.

"This place is huge. You have all this space to yourself?"

"No. My sister, Annie, lives with me. Or, really, I live with her. She's the moneymaker out of the two of us."

"Sister? And she's…"

"At work." Logan smiled.

"Not that it, you know, matters if anyone else is here. Since this isn't a date and all." Connor quickly erased the subtle hint of lust that tinged her voice.

"Right. Absolutely not a date."

"And I will certainly not be sleeping with you again." Connor took a seat on a nearby breakfast stool and crossed her arms.

"Whoa. Who's talking about sleeping together? I just wanted to make you dinner."

Connor let her face soften into a quiet smile and squeezed Logan's hand. "I still don't really believe you can cook. You know that, right?"

Logan continued to dance around the kitchen, pulling out spices and pots and pans. "Always so quick to judge. You really think all firefighters are just dumb lugs, don't you?"

"Not all." Connor furrowed her brow. "Just most."

"For the record," Logan said, opening a bottle of cooking wine and flipping through her iPod, "I'm neither dumb nor a lug." She settled on one of Connor's favorite bands.

"The Smiths, huh? I guess I don't hate your taste in music."

"You know what I think?" Logan stopped for a minute and gave Connor a long, smoldering look that made her face tingle with a rush of heat. "I think you wildly underestimate me."

Connor smiled, momentarily content to let Logan prove to her just how wrong she'd been.

"So what are you making?"

"Steak tenderloin with a turnip mash and a wine reduction." Connor's jaw hung limply in the air. "Oh, shit. I'm such an asshole. I forgot to ask if you eat meat! And red meat at that! I just assumed that—"

Connor got up from her seat and moved toward Logan until their bodies were almost touching, the heat between them so palpable that a cold sweat formed around her collar. Her breath came faster, and it took every bit of restraint she had not to reach out and brush the hair from Logan's flushed cheek. But she couldn't. Not when Logan looked so good. Not when it would be so easy to slip into the want that consumed her when she was around.

"It's okay. I'm not a vegetarian. I love steak." She smiled coyly before realizing she was crossing a dangerous line and took a cautious step away from Logan. She could be cordial to her. Kind even. But that was it. Anything more was too much of a risk, and touching her would surely be the end of any kind of rational thought.

"I still can't believe what happened today," Connor said.

Logan brought the steaming dishes to the table and sat down next to her. "Neither can I."

"You know, in all my years on the streets, I've never been shot at. In fact, I don't think I've ever been in any real kind of danger. Just the usual pissed-off drunk or combative diabetic. But nothing like that."

"I had a couple of run-ins in Chicago," Logan said casually.

"What do you mean? Don't tell me this isn't the first time you've been shot at."

Logan looked away. "There were two other times."

"Two?!" Connor stared at her across the table, her head cloudy with anger and distrust. This was why she couldn't, why she wouldn't, touch Logan again. This was why she wouldn't let her in. Loss was almost inevitable when you lived this way.

"It wasn't a big deal. I'm fine. Really." Logan rubbed her left arm.

"Oh my God. You were shot! Someone shot you! Not just *at* you. They actually…Oh my God!"

"Connor." Logan got up and crossed to her side, kneeling down next to her. "It was nothing. Barely needed stitches."

Without warning, Connor's eyes burned and filled with hot tears. "What the hell's wrong with you?!"

"Calm down." Logan put her arm around Connor's shoulder and pulled her close. "I'm right here. It was a long time ago."

Connor sniffled a couple more times and composed herself, keeping her tone stoic and her body still. "At least tell me what happened."

"Okay. I was off duty. It was early Saturday morning and I stopped by a little convenience station in this seedy neighborhood in Lincoln Park. I was at the register when this guy came in, waving a gun around and screaming nonsense. He told me to get down, but I…well…I didn't…"

Connor's heart shattered like glass.

"I tackled him. He got a shot off, and it grazed my left arm. It was just long enough for the clerk to grab his gun from behind the counter and take him down."

"Jesus, Logan."

"I know it was stupid. And crazy. And I know it may look like I make really awful choices sometimes. But I swear I'm not like that anymore." Logan ran her hand through Connor's hair.

"Really?"

"Yes. I swear."

"Is that why you ran back into that building a few weeks ago after everyone told you not to?"

"That was—"

"Stupid. Dangerous. Careless, Logan. God, it's no wonder I don't want to get close to you if you're going to...Never mind."

"No. Tell me what you wanted to say."

Connor's anger grew until she jumped to her feet, ready to run as fast and far as she could away from the possibility of loss. Away from Logan.

"You're not invincible, you know. And you really are just a lug. I knew you were no different than..." Kam's face filled her vision.

"Kam?" A heavy silence flooded the kitchen. But instead of running, Connor let her anger deflate, and she collapsed back onto the chair.

"Yes."

"I'm sorry. I don't know anything about Kam. Forgive me?"

"You're right. Kam was reckless too. Always had to be the hero. Everyone else came first. It was what I loved about her. It was also what killed her."

"Connor, we don't have to talk about—"

"No. I want to. I don't hate firefighters because I think they're big idiots who try to kill my patients. I hate firefighters because they're constantly tempting death. And if I let you...I mean, if I let anyone else in again...I just can't do that."

Logan smiled sweetly at her. "I understand. I really do."

"You do?" Connor's chest tightened.

"I do. No one chooses to go into a burning building without accepting that they might not come out. And, as hard as that is for us, it's even harder for the people who love us."

"How about you then, Logan Curtis? Who loves you?"

Logan was silent for a minute, then shrugged. "Annie. And I suppose my parents loved me once upon a time. You know, before I told them I liked girls."

"Oh, I'm sure plenty of women have loved you too." Connor didn't want to care so much, but she found herself having to know just how many women had fallen for Logan. Or, worse, how many of them Logan had loved.

"I haven't been in a real, honest-to-God relationship since I was...I don't know, twenty-three?"

"What?"

"Oh, fuck. Why am I telling you this again?" Logan laughed self-consciously.

"Because. I make you disgustingly honest." She smiled.

"You do." Logan brushed her fingers against Connor's face.

"You can't really tell me you've just been sleeping around for the last ten years."

"I...uh..."

"You have been. Jesus." Connor suddenly wasn't sure whether to be relieved or terrified that Logan had never really been in love.

"I mean...I haven't slept around *that* much." Logan blushed, and something about the vulnerability in her eyes comforted Connor's distrust.

"I want to see it."

"Huh? See what?"

"Your shoulder...the scar."

Logan stood slowly and Connor followed. She watched as Logan began to unbutton her shirt, their gazes fused. Connor had almost forgotten how beautiful she was. Almost. But with every inch of skin she bared, it was becoming impossible not to remember. Her skin tingled and her legs tensed, and she wanted to trace her fingers down the lines of Logan's stomach and on to the buckle of her belt. She couldn't, though. If she did, she wouldn't be able to go back. Logan slid her arms out of her sleeves and revealed a small, quarter-sized scar on her left shoulder.

"I told you it's not a big deal. It just grazed me."

"Logan," Connor whispered, touching the hard, thick skin. "Please. Be careful."

"What? I'm always careful."

"I'm begging you. When everyone else is running away from something, promise me you will too."

"I..." Logan looked at her, her face seemingly trying to convey what her words couldn't. Connor knew it was too much to ask of someone like Logan. Even Kam couldn't do this for her.

"You know what?" Connor turned and looked at the wall, suddenly feeling stupid and out of line. "It's not any of my business. I'm sorry."

A key rattled in the door and a tall, pretty woman with Logan's black hair walked in and tossed her purse haphazardly on the floor.

"Oh, shit," Annie said.

"Annie..." Logan dropped to the floor and grabbed her shirt, tossing it over her bare torso.

"I'm so sorry. I didn't know you had company and obviously I'm interrupting and...Hi." Annie smiled kindly at Connor. "I'm Annie." She held out her hand.

"I'm Connor. It's so nice to meet you." She returned the gesture.

"Well, Connor," Annie winked at Logan, "I'll be leaving you two alone now. Again, so sorry to interrupt."

Not until Annie had disappeared down the hall did Connor notice the crimson color Logan's skin had taken on.

"That was my sister, apparently home early. Great."

"It's not a problem. Really. A little unfortunate she had to walk in when she did, but definitely not a problem."

"You're pretty phenomenal, you know that?"

Now it was Connor whose face burned. "Oh, stop. Dinner was wonderful, by the way. Thank you." And Connor meant it. She had to admit she hadn't expected much of Logan. Time and again, she'd placed her in a box, assuming she knew exactly who she was and what she was capable of. And time and again, she'd been wrong. Logan could cook. That was a surprise in and of itself. But the company she'd provided over dinner was even more unanticipated. Connor was getting dangerously fond of being around her. She touched Logan's arm.

"I told you I wasn't the degenerate you thought I was."

"Yes, well, that remains to be seen." Connor grinned and allowed Logan to put her hand on her lower back. Being touched by Logan felt all too good, even when it shouldn't have.

"I'll walk you out."

"Thank you. Tonight was…it was really nice." Her eyes held Logan's, and she momentarily gave in to temptation, pressing her body against hers and circling her arms around Logan's neck. It was suicide to get so close to Logan, but she did it anyway. Her musk that brought back flashes of their night together wafted through the electric air, and her hands on Logan's shoulders warmed her all the way through. A few more seconds in her arms couldn't hurt. Could it?

"I had a great time."

"I'll, uh…see you around then?"

"Yeah. See you around."

Connor walked out into the street, cursing herself all the way. *See you around? What is wrong with you?!* But really, what else could she say? It's not like she could make plans to see Logan again. No. That was impossible. All she could do was secretly hope their paths would cross and try as hard as she could to stop thinking about her.

❖

"Tell me everything," Annie said, running into the kitchen so quickly her socked feet skidded on the hardwood floor. Logan still stood in the doorway, willing Connor to come back and kiss her, or touch her, or tell her she wanted to stay the night. "Staring at the door won't make her appear again, little sis."

"Huh?" Logan shook her head, pulling herself away from her daze.

"You are a sad…sad case." Annie poured a glass of the wine that Logan had left out and sat on the stool Connor had occupied.

"I don't know what you mean."

"This girl really has something on you. I mean, I can see why. She's hot. But holy hell, Loge, what's gotten into you?" Logan sat down beside her and let her head collapse into her hands.

"Oh, God, I don't know, Annie. I really don't know. I've never felt like this before. It's bad."

Annie smiled and squeezed her hands together, clearly pleased with her sister's state of infatuation. "It's not bad. It's perfect. It's…You're in love with her. I never thought I'd see the day. But here it is. You're actually in love."

"Settle down. I'm not saying I'm 'in love.' I just…she's different. She's the only girl I've ever met who's made me want to stop fucking around. She makes me want to give it a try, you know, a relationship." Logan felt her face fall.

"So what's the problem?"

"The problem?"

"Yeah. The problem. I know you well enough to know when there's a catch. What's keeping you and Connor from trying?"

"Nothing. Why?"

"Because she took off out of here without so much as a good-night kiss and left you with those sad little puppy eyes."

"You were watching us?" Logan scoffed.

"You're damn right I was watching. Listen, Loge. I know you think you're infallible. You think you're this rock-hard badass who can't be penetrated by anyone. But that's not what I saw back there. What I saw is a girl who has my baby sister's heart in her hand already. You're the one who needs to be protected now."

❖

"Sorry, were you sleeping?" It was three a.m., and Connor was tired of fidgeting in bed thinking about Logan.

"Actually…No," Jake said, the grogginess evident through the phone. "Parker's been up all night with a cold. Laurie's got it too, so that makes me Mr. Mom."

"Apron and everything?"

"What do you need, Haus?" She could nearly hear Jake smiling.

"I had dinner at Logan's tonight."

"I know. I was at the station when…wait…*at* Logan's? As in, at her house?"

"Yes. Her house."

"So you did *it* again."

"No, Jake, we didn't 'do it.' That's the scary part. We didn't do anything. We just…talked. She was…perfect."

"Perfect?" Jake's voice perked up.

"You know, perfectly behaved. That's what I meant."

"Come over."

"I'll bring the snacks."

❖

Twenty minutes later Connor hopped out of a cab in front of Jake and Laurie's familiar two-family home in Somerville. It wasn't the first time she'd shown up there at some ungodly hour. Right after Kam died, it became a nearly weekly occurrence. As she turned the key she had retrieved from its hiding place under a broken piece of tile under the mailbox, she thought she didn't have many friends in this world, but Jake was probably worth about a hundred.

"Shhh, Parker's finally down," Jake whispered as he met her at the door. His eyes were rimmed red but gleaming with a pride that had been there since their baby was born. Fatherhood suited him. Connor wondered if she'd ever get the chance to have a kid of her own, before her eggs became too old and shriveled and useless. No. That would involve actually meeting someone worth raising a family with. Or rather, someone she was willing to trust enough to have a life with.

"Sorry."

"Come in. Let's go to the living room. I don't want to bother Laur."

She followed Jake into the tiny living room she'd spent countless hours in and sprawled out on the couch she'd slept on a dozen times after Kam died. Most nights, she'd been fine alone. In fact, Connor had preferred it. She could lie in bed with Rusty, wearing Kam's BU T-shirt that still smelled like her, no matter how many times it had been washed since, and listen to every Elliot Smith album ever made. Sure, it was depression that bordered on Sylvia Plath-scary, but it got her through. Some nights, though, it wasn't enough. So she'd call Jake or, even more often, just show up at their apartment and cry herself to sleep on the sofa. Somehow, it was better knowing people who loved her were in the next room. As long as Jake and Laurie were sleeping safely next to her, they couldn't leave her too.

"Tell me what happened." Jake tore open a bag of Doritos, trying not to let the sound of the crinkling packaging travel down the hall to his sleeping family.

"I already told you. Nothing happened. That's just it."

"I'm surprised. Logan's such a player. You know I was walking past that crappy bar, the Crow's Nest, the other night on the way home from a diaper run, and I saw her leave with…" He must have noticed Connor's mouth curling into a scowl. "Never mind. It must not have been her. It must have been someone else I saw."

"What did you see, Jake?"

"Nothing. It must have just been someone that looked like Logan."

"Jacob Patrick O'Harrigan, tell me what you saw, or I swear to God I will go in there right now and wake up that beautiful, sleeping wife and baby of yours and tell them it was your fault."

"No. No, don't do that. Parker's been screaming all night. I don't know how that kid has any air left in him. And Laurie is so grumpy when she's sick. Please. I'll tell you."

"Good."

"The night of our last shift with Logan, after you so kindly told her to go screw off, I was walking past the Crow's Nest, and I saw this girl. Normally, I try to get the hell out of that area as fast as I can. But I stopped when I saw a BFD logo on the girl's shirt. She looked a lot like Logan. There was someone with her. This cute little redhead in a long coat with big shoes. She was hanging all over her. They stopped and…" Jake turned away from her, "kissed a little. And then they took off."

Connor's heart clenched, and she was overwhelmed by a sickening sense of disappointment that blindsided her. "You're sure it was Logan?"

"I'm sure, Haus."

Connor composed herself, shaking her head as if to disassemble any feelings of hurt that had settled in her at the thought of Logan taking home some one-night stand. And so soon after their night together too. "It's fine. Really. No big deal. I mean, Logan doesn't owe me anything, right? It's not like we're dating. It's not like it meant anything. It was just sex."

Jake raised his eyebrows in seeming disbelief.

"You want to know what I think?"

"Not really, no."

"You're here, aren't you? So you must want to."

Connor scooped up a handful of chips and gnawed on them, glaring at Jake. "Fine. What do you think?"

"She likes you. A lot."

"So how do you explain her lady of the night then, huh?"

"I don't know Logan very well. But I have a theory."

"Of course you do." Connor scoffed.

"Just listen. I have a theory. People like Logan use sex almost like...like alcoholics use a drink."

"Wait...are you suggesting Logan's a...sex addict?!"

"No! I don't think it meant anything, that girl from the other night."

"And what makes you say that?" Connor asked, trying to hide her growing excitement.

"You're going to make fun of me for this. But she didn't look at this girl the way she looked at you."

"You're such a sissy." Connor threw a pillow at his head.

"I mean it. It was different. When she kissed her, it was empty. Even from where I was standing I could see that. Nothing like how she was with you at the gala."

"You realize how stupid all this sounds, don't you? You're telling me you think Logan took some bar-trash home and slept with her because she likes me?"

"Yes. Exactly. You rejected her, Haus. And I know I wasn't the only one who saw the hurt in her face when you did. So she did the only thing people like Logan know how to do to make the hurt stop. She hit the bedroom with a stranger. A stranger who could never hurt her."

Connor thought about it for a minute. A long shot? Maybe. But she couldn't help but like the idea of Logan's tryst being nothing more than a temporary escape from the memory of their time together. She couldn't help but like the idea that Logan might actually, honestly, care about her.

"Even if that's true, it doesn't really matter, does it? I don't like her like that. We shared one amazing, sexy-as-hell evening together, and that was it. So I don't loathe her anymore? So there was a spark? Obviously, whatever it was is done. She didn't even try to kiss me tonight." Connor couldn't help the frustration that crept into her voice.

"And that drives you crazy, doesn't it?" Jake smirked his knowing smirk that reminded Connor there was no putting anything over on him. There never had been. He knew her too well. He loved her too much.

"No. Of course not. Why would I care?"

"Because you still want her."

"I do not."

"You do. You want those big BFD hands all over you again. 'Oh, Logan, don't stop. Oh, Logan.'" Jake was nearly hysterical now.

"Shut up! You're such a child!" But Connor couldn't resist letting a small smile creep onto her face.

"When are you going to learn? I'm right. About everything."

Connor sighed and sank back farther into the couch. "And what if you are? What if I do still think she's kind of attractive? Why didn't she make even one single pass at me tonight?"

"Because," Jake said, his eyes getting heavy, "she likes you. You're different. She doesn't want to treat you like any other one-nighter. She's…Christ, I think she's trying to court you." Connor laughed.

"Court me? I don't think Logan Curtis 'courts' anyone."

"Hey," Jake yawned, "there's a first for everything, isn't there?"

❖

When Connor woke up, she was still on Jake's couch, and someone had put a fleece blanket over her legs. Jake was drooling next to her, the same blanket barely covering his feet. She rubbed her eyes and sat up slowly.

"Morning, sunshine." Laurie sat at the kitchen table drinking a cup of coffee and feeding Parker, who bounced giddily in his high chair.

"Hey, Laurie."

"Rough night?" She smiled tenderly at Connor.

"Just confusing I guess. I wasn't planning on staying. I hope it's okay—"

"You know you're always welcome here. Always. But next time, feel free to push Jacob onto the floor. He tends to snore like a foghorn."

"Trust me, I've noticed."

"Everything okay? The last time you spent the night here was..." Laurie stopped, turning back to her son and wiping pureed carrots off his chin.

"Yeah. Everything's fine. I mean, no one's dead, if that's what you're asking." Connor let out a small laugh and Laurie visibly relaxed.

"Is it that hottie firefighter again?"

"You mean Logan?" Connor got up and crossed to the table, stopping to tickle Parker's round belly.

"Coffee?"

"Please." Laurie poured her a cup from a nearly empty pot that was already waiting next to her.

"You won't believe how much of this stuff we've gone through since Parker was born. I swear we should buy stock in Folgers."

Connor smiled cordially.

"So tell me what she did."

"Nothing, really. I agreed to have dinner with her. You know, after the shooting yesterday."

Laurie's eyes widened. "The what?!"

"Oh…um…There was just this little thing yesterday with a patient. Nothing major. Jake will tell you all about it."

"You bet your ass he will. You know what? Never mind. I don't think I want to know. You're all okay, right?"

"We're fine."

"Good. Then I'll just pretend I didn't hear that. So she took you to dinner."

"Kind of. She told me she was taking me to 'the best place in town.' Next thing I knew, we were in her kitchen."

Laurie laughed. "Oh, she is smooth, isn't she?"

"That's part of the problem, I think…"

"Did you, you know?"

"No. Not even a kiss. We just talked. About our pasts and our families…everything. I told her things I haven't told anyone besides you and Jake."

"Connor, that's fantastic." Laurie smiled in approval.

"Not exactly. I mean, this was what I wanted, right? For her to leave me alone? To stop this little fling we started?"

"I'm listening."

"This was what I wanted. So why do I feel so shitty?"

Laurie reached out and squeezed her hand. "Because sometimes what your head wants isn't what your heart wants. You're a smart girl. You can tell the two things apart."

"That's the problem. I'm not so sure I can."

## CHAPTER TWELVE

"Medic 884, bravo-echo-nine, respond to the Shillman Arena at 4039 Center Street for a twenty-year-old male, hit his head while ice skating. Over."

By the time Jake could get to the mic on the station wall, Connor was already in the front seat of the rig.

"884 responding to Shillman Arena. Over."

"884, be advised Engine 19 is already on scene with the patient." Connor's always-steady heart rate doubled.

"Copy that. Over."

"Looks like we'll be seeing your knight-in-shining-bunker-gear then, huh?" Jake slapped her shoulder while he steered the ambulance out of the garage.

"Shut it, O'Harrigan." But Connor looked out the window and smiled to herself. By the time they'd pulled up to the skating rink a few minutes later, Connor hadn't finished putting together her plan for her newest patient. In fact, she hadn't even begun. Every time she started going over head-injury protocols, Logan's face showed up. That thick, black hair and those icy blue eyes. Those two ever present asymmetrical dimples. *Pull it together, Connor.*

Jake loaded up the stretcher and Connor took the gear bag inside.

"Careful, it's slippery," Logan shouted from the middle of the now nearly deserted ice rink. A gaggle of BFDs surrounded what Connor could only guess was the patient, each of them in full turnout gear, a slew of bandages and blood pressure cuffs and splints in their wake.

"I played hockey for fifteen years," Connor responded dryly, sliding gracefully to Logan's side.

"Forgive me. I forgot who I was talking to." But the banter was lacking its usual hint of anger and distaste. Logan allowed her a long, smooth smile and Connor's insides tumbled.

"What's the story?"

"This is Mark. Say hi, Mark." The young man strapped to the backboard grinned up at her.

"Tell me the cute one gets to ride with me to the hospital," Mark said. Logan laughed wildly.

"I'm Connor, Mark. I'm a paramedic. What happened?"

"Nothing much. I just took a digger. Hit my head. I'm okay though. These jerks strapped me onto this thing anyway."

"These aren't jerks," Connor said, lightly. "They're the good guys. I promise."

Marty Taylor took a step toward the group. "Can we go on record with that one, Haus?" he said.

"Settle down, Taylor. What do you think? We're all going to hold hands and sing folk songs now?"

"Take good care of this one," Taylor said. "He's my baby brother's best friend."

"Thanks, Marty," Mark responded.

"We will. Don't worry. Mark, we're going to get you over to the hospital, okay? Everything looks fine. But we just need to make sure."

"Can we use the sirens?"

"Probably not, no."

Jake, Taylor, and Logan loaded Mark into the rig, and Connor jumped in the back.

❖

Dr. Galen Burgess was sitting in the nurses' station of the Boston City ER, one hand gripping a cup of coffee and the other in the hair of a pretty, young brunette who laughed eagerly at whatever it was she said. Logan despised her. Probably partly because she saw too much of herself in Galen. But mostly, because every time she looked at her, she saw her touching Connor. She saw her bronzed, smooth skin on top of Connor's, her experienced, selfish hands on her body, her slimy little grin aimed at her beautiful face…

"Logan, what are you doing here, bud?" Galen turned briefly from the girl who was now nearly in her lap.

*Bud? I'm not your bud, you prick.*

"Did 884 show up yet?"

"Who's 884?" Galen said, quickly seeming to lose interest in Logan's presence and returning to finger the girl's ID badge while she flashed her doe eyes at her.

"Connor's rig." Galen perked up a little at Connor's name, but then turned away. "Connor and Jake, I mean. They're supposed to be bringing a patient in. A kid with a concussion."

"Nope. Pretty dead in here right now." And with that, Logan had lost her. Galen was fully absorbed with her newest conquest, and Logan was left standing like a lost idiot.

"Look alive, Dr. B. Incoming." Logan knew Jake's voice even without turning around. Galen sighed loudly, plastered on her most practiced smile, and reluctantly got up from her post.

"What do you have for me today, guys?"

"Are you my doctor?" Mark said, still strapped tightly to the stretcher.

"That's what they tell me. I'm Dr. Burgess. But you can call me Galen." She winked at him and Logan turned, disgusted.

"But you can call me Galen," she mimicked quietly in a nasally chirp.

"Everything all right over here?" Connor said, coming up behind her.

"Huh? Oh yeah. Everything's cool. Real great."

Jake and Galen continued wheeling Mark down the hall to the exam room.

"Good. What are you doing here, anyway, Logan?"

"You know I like to follow up on my patients." She lied. She used to be a good liar. Great even. Add that to the list of things that were changing for Logan.

"Right. Well, that's sweet of you. Tell Taylor that Mark will be fine. I'll make sure Galen takes good care of him."

Logan felt her face twist in disdain.

"What? What's the matter?"

"What? Oh, nothing. You better catch up to them...I bet Jake's already halfway through a Parker story by now. I'm going to go get some coffee." She smiled at Connor, silently kicking herself for letting her go. Logan didn't exactly have a plan in mind. But she'd hoped by the end of their conversation, she'd find a way to see Connor again.

Logan was halfway through her cup of coffee in the Boston City charting room when Connor finally approached. But she wasn't alone. Galen was tightly in tow, her sickeningly charming grin accompanied by a glint in her eye that said she knew she was about to get some, and that Connor was her next target. As they walked, her hand drifted to the small of Connor's back, and Connor stopped and playfully straightened the lapel on Galen's pristine white coat. Logan heard herself groan.

"We have to go," Connor said, and gently pinched Galen's shoulder.

"I'll call you?"

"No, you won't." She smiled, hailed Jake from down the hall, and walked toward the automatic doors without so much as a glance Logan's way. When Connor was well out of her line of sight, Galen picked up her cell phone, smiling wryly at what was surely some other girl's flirtatious message. Before she turned the corner to go, Logan was there, in front of her.

"Can I talk to you for a minute, Galen?"

"Sure. What's up?"

"Connor. You. That's 'what's up.' Isn't it?"

"I thought we covered this already, bro."

Logan rolled her eyes.

"Not really, no. And I'm not your 'bro'. Now tell me what's going on with you and Connor. Do you like her?"

Galen balked. "Do I like her?"

"Yes. Do you like her? Or is that a foreign concept to you?"

"Look. I'm just having fun here, okay? I don't know what you're on my case about."

"No, you look." Logan was towering over the much smaller Galen, and her voice was suddenly fierce. Galen took several steps back, glancing nervously around the department. "Connor Haus isn't the kind of girl you just have fun with. She's special. Trust me. She likes you. Don't fuck this up." She shot Galen one last hard look and was gone.

It was late in the afternoon by the time Connor made it back to Boston City's ER. After handing off a middle-aged man with chest pain to one of the other residents, she grabbed a Diet Coke from the lounge and restocked her bag, mentally exhausted from a long shift, but more from constantly thinking about Logan.

"Can we talk?" Galen approached her timidly—something Connor had never seen before.

"Sure. What is it?" She stopped what she was doing, suddenly gravely concerned about whatever it was that had Galen so worked up.

"McLug the Firefighter. What's her deal?"

"You mean Logan?" Connor's pulse tripped like it seemed to do every time she said Logan's name.

"That's the one. She basically threatened to bash my face in earlier today."

"She what?!"

"Okay, well, maybe not that extreme. But she did say a couple of things…about you."

"She did?" Connor did her best to sound only minimally interested. "What did she say?"

"Well, she wanted to know what was going on between us. I told her we were just having fun and she should back off. Then she got really pissed and told me 'Connor Haus isn't the kind of girl you just have fun with. She's special. Trust her.'"

"She said that?" Connor couldn't help but smile.

"Yeah. Look, Connor, if I'm getting in the middle of anything…"

"You're fine, Galen. It's nothing. Really."

"If that was nothing to her, I'd sure hate to see what something looks like."

Connor turned and left, still smiling the entire way back to the rig.

❖

Logan didn't want to go home yet. She was angry and hurt and sexually frustrated from all the ways she'd been remembering having Connor. And she wanted to slap the shit out of Galen Fucking Burgess. Just having fun? Who did she think she was, anyway? A perfect tan and a great head of hair don't entitle you to play with the hearts of girls like Connor. She walked the five blocks from the bus station, the early spring night warmer than most. She traced the edges of her cell phone with her fingers inside her jacket pocket. She thought about calling Connor. More than anything she wanted to feel her again, even if it was just once more. But Connor didn't want her. She'd told Logan this much time and time again. She wanted Galen. Or, at least, that was how it looked.

She thought about going home, but the door to the Crow's Nest was propped open, with the familiar bouncer who knew her by name waiting out front, and she thought what would be the harm in a whiskey and a little company.

"Makers, Sandi. Hell, better make it a double tonight." Logan crashed down onto the bar stool and shrugged out of her leather jacket.

"Ever heard of manners, sweetheart?" Sandi the bartender slid a cocktail napkin in front of her.

"Is that a new kind of whiskey?"

"Oh, you are in a mood tonight. Come on, handsome. What's the deal?" The place was quiet, and Sandi took a minute to prop her elbows up on the bar and wait.

"Nothing."

"Someone die today at work or something?" Sandi was prying.

"No. Nothing like that." She took a sip of her drink, savoring the burn as it slid down her throat.

"Girl problems, then."

"Yeah. Guess so."

"Now tell me what kind of girl problems a Casanova like you has. I see you in here at least twice a week. You come in alone, but you never leave alone. So what is it about this one that's got you so miserable?"

Logan sighed and put down the glass.

"She's different. I know I keep saying that, but she just is. She's got something on me. And she doesn't seem to know I'm alive. Or at least doesn't seem to care." Out of the corner of her eye she noticed a blonde with a short pixie cut in an unseasonable strapless top sitting by the jukebox. If she couldn't forget about

Connor forever, she could at least find someone to take her mind off her for a few hours. "Excuse me, Sandi." Logan got up and took her drink to the back of the bar where the pixie girl sat alone.

"Where you going, sweetheart?" Sandi called. When she noticed where Logan was heading, she shook her head. Logan appreciated that people like Sandi and Annie cared so much. But she was also tired of everyone trying to save her from herself.

"The music on this thing is horrible. I think the last time they updated it was 1984." Logan smiled at the girl and tossed a couple of quarters into the jukebox.

"I noticed. I think I saw White Snake on there at least fifteen times."

"Oh, at least. And several versions of 'Every Rose Has its Thorn' too."

The girl grinned and held out her hand.

"I'm Holly."

"Logan. What are you drinking, Holly?"

"Old-fashioned, with ginger ale."

"So it's a girly old-fashioned then."

"I call it an Old-Fashioned Girl, actually. It's sort of my signature."

Logan liked her. She was funny, and easy, and something about her voice was airy and light. They talked for hours, drinking whiskey and taking turns picking outdated rock ballads. Logan thought Holly might be the kind of girl she could spend some time with—the kind of girl she could get to like. But then, Connor came to mind. Not that Connor had ever really left her mind to begin with. No. She'd been there the whole time. Holly was just a distraction. And she definitely wasn't Connor.

"I'm having a really good time with you, Logan. But I think I better get going," Holly finally said, touching Logan's arm.

"I know this is a little weird, but I live right up the street if you wanted to come over and have another drink or something…"

Holly smiled at her shyly and paused a minute. Then she leaned in and kissed her softly, her lips just fluttering over Logan's.

"You know what?" she said. "That sounds great."

"Perfect. Let's go."

As Logan unlocked the front door to her apartment, a pit opened in her stomach. It was only one of dozens of times she'd brought a girl she hardly knew back to her place. But it was the first time she felt sick about it. She pushed the discomfort back down, taking Holly's hand and leading her inside. Annie was in bed already. Logan knew she would be. So many nights of meaningless sex had taught her exactly how to get what she wanted without interruption.

"Nice place," Holly said, taking off her coat and handing it to Logan.

"Thanks. How about another drink?"

"Love one." She placed her soft hands on Logan's shoulders and kissed her, sweetly, sensually. But Logan felt nothing.

"What is it?" Holly pulled away.

"What do you mean?"

"You." She slid her fingers up under Logan's shirt. "I can tell when a girl's not into me."

"I doubt you've ever met a girl who isn't into you."

"Tell me what's going on then."

Logan responded by cupping her face in her hands and kissing her again, her frustration and angst attempting to transform into something resembling passion.

"Nothing's going on," she said, finally pulling away. The usual tightening in her thighs and drum roll in her chest were nowhere to be found. What *was* going on?

"Good. Then why don't you show me where your bedroom is." Holly smiled coyly and fingered the button of Logan's jeans. A quiet rapping at the door made Logan jump. She hadn't realized how tense she'd been.

"Sorry. I have no idea who this could be. Sometimes some of my fire buddies think it's okay to drop by drunk in the middle of the night." She opened the door, her heart sinking to her feet.

"Connor." The silence lasted so long and was so agonizing, Logan had nearly forgotten about Holly.

Connor finally spoke, her voice shaky with anger and humiliation. She probably should have guessed showing up at Logan's place at one a.m. was a horrible idea. She probably should have guessed Logan Curtis wouldn't be alone.

"I'm sorry...I didn't know you had company..." She turned to leave, wanting to escape the tension, and the pretty girl standing behind Logan, as quickly as possible.

"No, wait." Logan grabbed her by the elbow, the mortification visible on her face. "We were just...This is..." She gestured to the girl behind her, but nothing else escaped her mouth.

"Holly." The pretty girl took a step forward until she was next to Logan and shook Connor's hand weakly.

"Nice to meet you, Holly. I was...I'll be going now."

"Don't." Logan's eyes were pleading.

"You know what?" Holly said. "I think I should be the one to go. It was nice to meet you, Logan." She gracefully moved toward the still-open door.

"I'll call you..." Logan stammered.

Holly smiled politely. "You were never going to call me, Logan. Good-bye."

Even after Holly had gone, Logan's face remained a deep red.

"This isn't how it looks," she said. "God, that sounds so cliché."

"Logan, it's fine. You don't have to explain anything. I shouldn't have just dropped by like this. It's the middle of the night. I must be crazy."

"No." She touched Connor's arm. "I'm happy you did. Really happy."

"I should go."

"What? You just got here. Why don't you come in? I'll get you a drink. Or I can cook something if you're hungry—"

"No. Thank you. But no. I just wanted to say..." Connor scrambled for excuses as to what she was doing there, but everything sounded pathetic and desperate. "Thank you. For dinner the other night. That's all."

"You came all the way here at one a.m. just to thank me for some steak?" Logan reached out to touch her again, but Connor pulled away.

"Yeah. I have to go. Sorry I ruined your date." Connor turned around and ran out the door, down the stairs, and onto the street, feeling foolish and hurt. Any half-baked idea she'd had of showing up at Logan's and reconnecting with her—letting her in—was ill-conceived and romanticized. And she once again succumbed to her old resolve.

## CHAPTER THIRTEEN

S tupid. Stupid, stupid, stupid…" Logan slapped her forehead with the palm of her hand.

"I'd say." When she opened her eyes again, Annie had appeared at the end of the hallway.

"What are you doing up?"

"I heard you making a mess of everything out here." She came up next to Logan and put her arm around her.

"I really fucked up."

"Yeah. You really did. What were you thinking, anyway?"

"Nothing!"

"That part's pretty clear." Annie rubbed her back.

"How was I supposed to know Connor would show up here in the middle of the night like that?"

"That's not the point. What were you doing bringing another bar-find back here? I thought you actually liked Connor."

"I do! So maybe I shouldn't have done that. But Connor made herself clear the other day. She doesn't want me. Besides, what was she doing here at one a.m.?"

Annie sighed and sat down at the bar stool Connor had occupied only a couple of nights earlier.

"You really are clueless aren't you?"

"Completely."

"Loge. She came because she likes you. Or at least she did before this little disaster. She likes you, and she was coming here to tell you. To give you a chance."

Logan's chest throbbed. "No. That's not it."

"Think about it, baby sis. No one shows up at someone's doorstep after midnight unless they want something. And that something is you." Annie stood up and walked back toward her bedroom.

"Wait. What do I do now?"

"Now?" Annie stopped. "Now you're going to have to try your best to get her back to where she was. And it's not going to be easy. Even for you. In fact, I'm not even sure it can be done."

Logan closed her eyes and exhaled hard. She'd get Connor back there, to wherever it was that brought her to Logan tonight. No matter what.

❖

Connor couldn't handle being alone after work the next night. So she'd strong-armed Jake into hitting up the Rose Bud for a couple of drinks and some games of darts. Not that it ever took too much strong-arming to get Jake to go out. He was desperate for a social life away from his wife and baby, who he loved more than he'd ever let on. And Connor knew he was also desperate for whatever it was she wanted to talk to him about. Jake cared for no one on this earth more than his family, and Connor. He wanted her to be happy. He wanted her with Logan.

"You really went there in the middle of the night," Jake repeated, as if he hadn't heard Connor correctly.

"Yes. I'm so humiliated. I just showed up at her door! And when I got there...Oh, God. I've never felt stupider, Jake. She was there with this girl. This really, really hot blond girl."

"Maybe it was her cousin?"

"Unlikely, seeing as she could hardly remember her name. It was obviously another one of Logan Curtis's little, what is it that you called them? Distractions? Well, she must really like me then. Because this is at least the second girl in the last couple weeks. Three, including me!" Connor shot a dart across the room as hard as she could, nearly taking off the tip of Jake's nose.

"I told you. This is how she is. You keep rejecting her, and she keeps trying to fill that void with girls who don't mean anything."

"What kind of sick excuse is that?"

Jake's eyes widened as she talked, and he cleared his throat dramatically, shaking his head toward the door. But Connor didn't take his cue.

"I don't care if she's so dysfunctional that she has to sleep around instead of getting to know me. That sounds like her problem. I'm done. What's the matter with you, anyway?"

"Ouch." Connor didn't need to turn around. She'd know the smoky tone of Logan's voice even in a dark room. "I wish I could pretend I didn't hear that."

Jake stood and rushed awkwardly to her.

"Hey, bud! What are you doing here?"

"Yeah, Logan. What are you doing here?" Connor refused to look at her.

"I just wanted to swing by after my shift and get a drink. Can we talk?"

"I'll just go…somewhere else," Jake said.

"No. Stay, Jake. I have nothing to talk to Logan about."

"Please?" Logan pleaded. "Just five minutes. Then I'll go. I promise."

"Your word doesn't mean a whole lot to me."

"Five minutes. That's all I need. And if you still want me to go, I will. I'll leave you alone. And you won't have to see my face again. Well, except on calls. I can't help…"

"Five minutes. That's it," Connor said. Jake smiled and walked to the bar.

"Okay." Logan sat down and Connor tapped coldly on her watch. "First of all, I lied to you."

"That's a shocker."

"I came here looking for you. I had to see you."

"Am I supposed to be charmed?"

"The other night, what you saw…" Logan went on.

"Oh, don't even try to tell me that girl was your cousin."

"What? No. She wasn't my cousin. She was nobody. I barely even got her name."

Connor let out a sarcastic laugh. "Nice. That really helps your case."

"Damn it. Let me start over. I don't want her, Connor. I don't want anyone but you. I never have, really. I know I haven't earned another chance with you, but I'll try. I'll do whatever it takes. Just give me a shot."

Connor looked at her for a long time, trying to quell the fire that had built in her belly.

"That's it? That's your big plea?"

"Well, yes," Logan said, seemingly defeated. "Please. Just let me take you out. One date. A real date. Let me show you that you can trust me."

"Trust you?" The fire inside Connor ignited until her blood was hotter than the desert sand. "How could I ever, in a million goddamn years, trust you, Logan? When you aren't running head-first into a burning building, you're sleeping with every girl south of 128! There is nothing, and I can't emphasize this enough, nothing about you that I can trust. Your five minutes is up. Now leave."

"But—"

"Go, Logan."

Finally, Logan got up and left, Connor's glare following her all the while.

"That was rough," Jake said, poking out from around the corner.

"Why am I even surprised that you were listening?"

"Yeah, you really shouldn't be by now." He sat down beside her and took a sip of his beer.

"I can't believe her."

"You can't believe her?"

"Yes! She follows us in here, admits to jumping in bed with that girl, and then asks me to trust her? What is wrong with her?"

"What's wrong with you?" Jake answered.

"Are you just going to repeat all my questions? Or are you actually going to contribute?" She slapped Jake on the back of his head.

"So she took another girl home? It's not like you'd given her any hope you'd ever get over yourself and come around."

"This is my fault?" Connor heard her voice rise.

"It's no one's fault, Haus. But Logan just bared her soul to you. Do you think that's something she makes a habit of? She wants to be with you."

"And how do I know she won't bring home anymore Hollys or whatever her name was? Or get herself killed like Kam doing something heroic and stupid? How do I know that, Jake? How could I ever possibly trust she'd actually come back to me at the end of the day?"

"How does anyone trust that? They just do. Because life's too miserable if you don't. Haven't you shut her out long enough?"

"No." Connor shook her head resolutely. "Not even close."

But Connor wondered if maybe she had shut Logan out long enough. Maybe Jake had a point. He did seem to be obnoxiously right about everything lately. Really, Logan owed Connor nothing. And she could take home all the girls in Massachusetts if she wanted. It wasn't like they were together. It wasn't like Connor had been anything but cold and horrible to her since they'd met. In fact, it was a near miracle that Logan still wanted her at all.

She stretched out on the sofa, and Rusty immediately pounced on her chest, purring and kneading her sweater. Connor picked up the novel she'd started from her coffee table and kicked off her boots. But she couldn't absorb a word. The only thing she saw on the pages were Logan's eyes as she had shouted at her earlier that afternoon. They were sad and wounded—things she never thought Logan was capable of feeling. Before she could give herself time to change her mind, Connor got up, threw her coat back on, and locked the door behind her, praying to God Logan was home.

❖

"One date," Connor said as Logan's apartment door creaked open. Annie stood in front of her.

"I'm flattered, but uh, I think you're looking for my sister."

Connor's heart lurched. "Oh God, I'm sorry. I really have a bad habit of embarrassing myself in this doorway, don't I?" She laughed nervously.

"Don't worry about it." Annie smiled and ushered her inside. "Logan's in her room. I'll go get her." Connor waited in the entryway, wondering exactly what she was doing there. This was a terrible idea. Nothing had changed. Logan was still a one-way ticket to a broken heart. But it was too late now. She was already at her door. She'd already let Logan in.

"Connor..." Logan said, hope emanating from her voice. She wore a loose Bruins T-shirt nearly sheer from years of use and a pair of running shorts that hung perfectly off her hips. Connor's throat tightened. She wasn't used to wanting anyone so much. It terrified her. But it also brought her back to a life she never thought she'd see again.

"Can we talk?"

"Of course. Anything you want." Logan put her hand timidly on Connor's shoulder, and Connor tried hard not to lose herself in how good it felt. "We can go for a walk maybe?"

"I'm going out, Loge," Annie said with a smile. "I won't be home until late. Very, very late. Good to see you again, Connor."

"Well. I guess we're alone…" Logan said, her usual poise replaced with uncertainty.

"I guess so." Connor smiled and took a couple of steps toward her, until she could put her hands on Logan's slim, inviting hips. Logan closed her eyes and sighed, seemingly savoring the chance to touch her.

"Do you want to come sit down? I mean, if you want…"

"I do."

"Okay." Logan led her into the living room, slowly, as if afraid any wrong move might break what was building between them. They sat down on the couch, Connor making no attempt to isolate herself. "Can I get you anything? Some wine? Beer? Water? I think I have some Diet Coke."

"I'm okay, Logan." Connor inched closer to her and put her hand on Logan's thigh, the warmth of her body radiating up her hand and down to her center. "I wanted to apologize."

"You?" Logan asked, incredulous.

Connor laughed. "Yes, me. What? You think I'm incapable of apologizing?"

"Of course not. I just don't think you have anything to apologize for." She covered Connor's hand with her own, letting their fingers intertwine.

"I was terrible yesterday. You don't owe me anything. We slept together. We had a great time." She shuddered at the memory of Logan's naked body on top of hers. "And I certainly had no right to make you feel badly for sleeping with anyone else."

"But I don't—"

"Shhh…" Connor brushed Logan's cheek and followed with her lips. "It doesn't matter. I don't care who you're sleeping with."

Logan's face fell a little as Connor tried to believe her own lie.

"You don't?"

"No." She leaned in slowly and kissed her, her hand resting gently on the back of Logan's neck. Connor melted into the sofa, her mind emptying of anything other than the way Logan's lips felt against hers. This could work, Connor told herself. This could work.

"So you'll go out with me?" Logan asked, eagerly, pulling away only a little, like she was worried Connor would try to leave again.

"Yes. I'll go out with you. But I don't want you thinking this is anything serious. I like you. You like me. That's all. I've had enough serious for a lifetime. Let's just go back to having a good time together, huh?"

"All right." Logan shook her head. "For now."

"For now?"

"Yeah. For now. But you see, Connor, that's not going to be enough for me forever. I want this. All of it. No one else."

Connor moved down the sofa, every cell in her body telling her to run as fast and as far as she could.

"But, until I can convince you that you want that too, I'll wait."

"You'll wait."

"I'll wait for you. I told you I'd do whatever it takes. And if that means I have to sleep with you, then by God I'll do it." She smiled wryly and Connor slid toward her again, climbing into her lap and kissing her harder, with more conviction.

"Oh, you poor thing," Connor whispered, her breath heavy now. Relief poured over her as the tension pulsed in her stomach.

Connor knew she wasn't any good at casual. But she had to be. Nothing else was an option.

## Chapter Fourteen

Connor woke up the next morning in a strange bed, wearing a strange T-shirt, with a strange smell coming from the next room. Eggs? Definitely eggs. And cheese. And bacon. An even better smell wafted off the empty pillow beside her, and she smiled, running the back of her hand down the sheets Logan had tangled herself in while she slept. It was dangerous to feel this good—in her room, her bed. And her stomach twisted in on itself, the feeling of imminent destruction suddenly overriding the musky pillow and dreamy early morning light streaming in through Logan's bedroom window.

"Good morning." Logan's smile was brighter than the approaching day as she nudged open the door with her knee, an overfilled tray teetering with breakfast food.

"Good morning yourself. And what is all this?"

"Breakfast, Your Majesty." She sat down on the bed next to her and placed the food between them.

"I thought we were keeping this simple," Connor objected, her heart stuttering in spite of herself.

"We are. Trust me, it's just scrambled eggs and bacon."

"Breakfast in bed is not simple, Logan. It's romantic. It's… well, it's not simple! It's the exact opposite of simple actually, it's—"

Logan picked up a piece of buttered bread and slid it into Connor's mouth as she spoke.

"Just breakfast." She smiled as Connor gave in and ate.

"So you do this for all your flings then, I take it?"

"Oh no."

Connor raised her eyebrows skeptically.

"They at least get pancakes. You and I are simple though. Just eggs."

"Good." But Connor wasn't sure why she suddenly wanted pancakes instead. She took another bite of toast and glanced at her cell phone. "Shit!"

She sprang to her feet.

"What is it?"

"It's 6:30? I never sleep that late!"

Logan grinned fiercely. "Yeah, well, we had a late night."

"Cute. But that doesn't change the fact that I'm late for my shift. And I don't have a uniform here. Damn it. I hate being late. I'm never late. I—"

"Hey." Logan stood and put her arms around her waist. "Relax. You must have a spare right?"

"Well yeah, at the station."

"So I'll give you something to wear until you get there."

Connor sighed and nodded, wondering how many seconds it would take until Jake figured out exactly what her night had looked like. Logan handed her a pair of jeans that were just a little too long and a T-shirt with the BFD insignia on the front.

"Don't you have anything else?" Connor asked, nervously.

"What's wrong? Worried about showing up to work in a BFD shirt?" Logan smiled. Connor could tell she was loving this.

"Of course not. That's stupid. Why would that matter? Okay, yes. Fine. Happy? Jake will never let me live this down. Are you sure you don't have another shirt?"

"Sorry." Logan grinned. "Laundry day."

❖

Connor hoped beyond hope she could get to the station and changed into a new uniform before Jake got there.

"Haus. You sneaky sonofabitch." But Jake was smiling wildly as he squatted near the rig, wiping down pieces of equipment.

"What?"

"Don't 'what' me. Nice shirt."

Connor felt her face burn, and she instinctively reached down and covered the BFD insignia.

"I don't suppose your bus broke down in front of station 51 last night and you were forced to spend the night with the fire department."

"No, Jake. And that's a really terrifying thought, thank you."

Abandoning his task, Jake sprang to his feet and rushed to Connor's side. "You have five seconds to start talking." He held up one hand.

"Or what?"

Jake dropped one finger, then another, and another. "Or I call over to station 51 and ask Logan herself what happened."

"She'll never talk."

"Ha! You did it! God, you're one confusing lady, Haus."

Connor sat down on the back of the rig, trying hard not to enjoy the feeling of Logan's T-shirt covering her shoulders and her breasts. Somehow, knowing it was hers kept the fire in her belly that had been there since the night before burning fiercely.

"Trust me, I know. I confuse myself."

"So what is it? You've forgiven her for Holly?"

Actually, Connor had nearly forgotten why she'd most recently been so insistent on keeping Logan at arm's length. But she silently told herself to thank Jake later for reminding her.

"Yeah, I guess I have."

"And you guys are finally together now? Thank God! I've been getting awfully tired of this will-they-won't-they bullshit!"

"First, no, we aren't. And second, no, you haven't. We're just spending time together. I don't want anything serious. And she understands that."

The corners of Jake's mouth fell into a scowl.

"She does."

"She does! Okay, well, she said…she said she'd 'wait for me.' But I mean, I think she gets it. For the most part. Maybe?"

"Holy shit, Haus." He dropped his forehead into his hands. "You're a hot mess. That's what I'm going to call you from now on. Connor 'Hot Mess' Haus. It suits you."

"What are you talking about?"

"You! You're crazy if you think that this isn't serious. She told you she'd wait for you, and you think you can get away with just the occasional roll in the sack? That girl has it bad for you. And you're going to break her heart if you don't admit to yourself that you have it bad too."

"You're wrong."

"Oh, I am? So when are you seeing her again then?"

"Tonight. She's taking me out to dinner at…"

"That's what I thought."

"It's nothing, Jake. It's just dinner."

"Sure thing." Jake slugged her on the shoulder. "Just dinner. Just a T-shirt. Just a little fun, right?"

"Exactly."

"Call it what you want, Haus. You can package it as nothing more than a sexy little sleepover. Or a simple hamburger. Or a borrowed T-shirt. But this is serious. It's serious whether you like it or not. And really, I think if you just gave it half a chance, you'd find you actually *do* like it." The tone rang through the station speakers, offering Connor a welcome distraction. But she hung on Jake's every word. God damn it, she hated it when he was right.

❖

An hour later, Jake backed the truck into the bay at Boston City, and Connor wheeled a young patient recovering from one of her regular seizures into the ER. She tried to keep her thoughts straight as she reported off to the team taking over, but the feeling of Logan's body against hers earlier that morning kept pulling her into a daydream, until she could just about hear Logan's voice trailing from down the hall. No. Not a crazy, lust-induced daydream this time. Logan was actually there.

As quickly as she reasonably could, Connor snuck off down the corridor of the ER, following the sound of Logan's now familiar and inviting tone. She had no plans as to what to say or do when she found her, but she didn't care. Logan stood near the wall, talking sternly with one of the nurses Connor knew well from years of bringing patients to Boston City. Connor couldn't make out what they were saying, but a few second later, Logan gently touched the nurse on the shoulder, smiled, and walked away.

The guys on the engine were already waiting for Logan in the cafeteria, but she didn't care. She liked to take a few minutes every shift to check on the patients she'd taken care of that week. Taylor and his goons would just have to deal with it. She was almost to the main lobby when someone reached out and grabbed at her hand, pulling her off her trajectory and through a cracked door. When she was finally able to look up and get her bearings, she was staring down into Connor's beautiful brown eyes, thick with need.

"Connor…" Logan smiled, the heat rising in her throat.

"Hi." She reached around Logan and shut the door to the tiny exam room, simultaneously sidling her body up against hers. Logan put her hands on Connor's waist and watched as she moved her lips onto hers, her senses flooded with Connor's soft perfume and the sound of her breath catching. Without any more words exchanged, they kissed until Logan's legs trembled and her stomach tightened, and Connor pulled handfuls of Logan's loose hair and gently bit her bottom lip.

"Damn it." Logan pulled away just enough, still holding Connor a breath away. "I have to meet the guys in the café. They're already waiting for me."

Connor kissed her again, slowly this time, until Logan's head swam to the ceiling.

"I understand. I'm still seeing you tonight, though, right?"

Logan brushed her cheek, hating that she had to leave right now.

"Wouldn't miss it." She kissed her again and left. Logan wasn't sure what had gotten into Connor. But she couldn't say she minded.

❖

"What? Stop looking at me like that. You're freaking me out."

Jake was sitting in the driver's seat, just staring at Connor expectantly.

"I'm not looking at you."

"Yes you are! You're doing it right now!" Connor turned and faced the window, knowing full well what Jake's problem was.

"Fine. I'm looking at you. Because I'm mad at you, Haus."

"Well, shoot. Should I call dispatch and ask for a transfer?"

"Like anyone else could put up with you." Jake turned on the radio, drumming on the dash as loudly as he could. Unable to stand what was Jake's annoying version of the cold shoulder, Connor turned down the music and faced him.

"Okay. I'll bite. Go ahead and get on your soapbox. You're going to anyway."

Jake's eyes lit up triumphantly and he puffed his chest.

"You can't go out with Logan tonight."

"I'm sorry?"

"You can't. You're going to break her heart."

Connor looked at him, perplexed.

"Hold on. I'm just trying to play catch-up here. You've spent the last few months basically forcing us together, and now you're telling me I can't go out with her."

"She's fragile, Haus."

Connor erupted with laughter. Imagine, Logan Curtis, fragile. This woman ran at burning buildings. She took bullets to the shoulder. No. Fragile was the last of Logan's traits.

"You're out of your damn mind."

"If you keep seeing her, or sleeping with her, or whatever it is you're doing—and please, spare me the details—she's going to get attached. You know what? Scratch that, she already is attached. She's going to fall for you, Connor. And you aren't in any shape to deal with that."

"I'm getting awfully tired of your opinions, you know that, don't you? Logan is a grown woman. I'm a grown woman. What we do is our problem. Why don't you let her decide just how involved she wants to get?"

Jake shook his head and tapped the steering wheel.

"Fine. But I'm not going to be here to clean up the mess you're about to make."

But she knew he would be. Jake would always be. Besides, if she was certain of one thing, it was that there was absolutely no chance of Logan falling in love with her.

# CHAPTER FIFTEEN

L ogan showed up at Connor's at eight p.m., but the truth was, she'd been pacing outside her apartment for half an hour. Maybe this was a mistake. After all, Connor had said she didn't want anything serious. What did that even mean, anyway? Logan used to know. For a long time the word serious wasn't even part of her vocabulary. She had no qualms about going from woman to woman, bed to bed, conveniently forgetting to call the next day. She had no problem forgetting about them. Not Connor. Logan couldn't forget about Connor if she tried. And, frankly, she didn't want to try. Logan liked thinking about Connor. She liked what she was becoming. Falling in love looked good on her.

"You look amazing." Logan's breath caught.

Connor stood in the door, wearing a short blue dress and strappy sandals, her dark-brown hair falling loosely down her shoulders. She looked Logan up and down for a long time, her eyes bright with want.

"Thank you." She smiled shyly and kissed Logan's cheek. "So where are you taking me?"

"Not to Chateau Curtis this time, if that's what you're asking."

Connor smiled, a hint of disappointment settling on her face.

"Too bad. I happen to like that place." She slid her hand inside Logan's leather jacket and down her back. "Maybe they have a room available after dinner?"

Logan's heart beat fitfully. As much as she wanted to get Connor back into her bed—as much as it had been all she'd thought about for days—she knew she had to play this differently. She had to win Connor over. She had to impress her. And it was going to take more than just phenomenal sex. Although that definitely couldn't hurt her cause.

"I think that could be arranged."

Logan led her across the street from Connor's building where her vintage Triumph waited patiently for them, nestled between two tightly parked cars.

"I thought you said you didn't have a motorcycle." Connor turned to her and grinned.

"I never said that. I said 'that shit's dangerous.' But so is fighting fires. And EMS, actually. At least motorcycles can't shoot you."

She knew it was a gamble bringing the bike. But she wanted Connor to know the truth—every truth about her.

"And you kept it hidden from me until you figured you'd successfully charmed your way into my pants?"

Logan tried to decipher the sparkle in Connor's eyes. "I didn't mean—"

"Logan," Connor circled her arms around Logan's neck and kissed her, the setting spring sun behind them highlighting the hues in Connor's hair. She was gorgeous. More than gorgeous, really. She was everything Logan never knew to want. "It's okay. My dad's been taking me out on his bike since I was a kid. And I hate to say this, since they're basically death traps with engines, but if it's at all possible...I think you just got sexier."

Logan's stomach tumbled.

"Just when I think I have you figured out..."

Connor kissed her again, slowly, holding onto her waist tightly. A warm breeze tousled Logan's hair, and Connor's sweet perfume that made her legs unsteady wafted through the air.

"You better be wearing a damn helmet."

Logan reached into a saddlebag and pulled out two, handing one to Connor with a smile.

"I'm not as reckless as you think," she said.

"Somehow, I doubt that."

But Connor might have thought differently had she known just how afraid Logan was to fall in love with her.

❖

Connor had never been to the tiny Mexican restaurant in the seaport that Logan took her to that night. In fact, she hadn't even known it existed. The waitress filled their water glasses, and Connor stared out the window at the lights over the harbor, her mind suddenly stuck on the image of the beautiful Holly standing innocently behind Logan a few days earlier. A flash of anger rose up in her, as she quietly reminded herself Logan was not hers. They were just having fun—exactly like Connor wanted.

But this wasn't really what Connor wanted. She looked at Logan, her painfully handsome face and impenetrable smile, and she wanted more. So much more. Of course, it didn't really matter what she wanted. What Connor wanted wasn't practical. She'd been alone for a long time now. The need would pass. Wouldn't it?

"What's the matter?" Logan reached across the table and took her hand.

"Nothing. What makes you think something's the matter?"

"Look, Connor, if you want to talk about the other night…"

Connor let out a boisterous chuckle. "What about the other night?"

"I promise you, Holly meant nothing."

"Oh, right. Holly. I actually forgot about that whole thing. Really."

Connor pulled her hand away and turned back to face the window, but Logan took her cheek in her hand, forcing her to look at her.

"Well, I didn't. You can call whatever this is between us anything you want. Call me your friend, your coworker, your friend-with-benefits. I don't care. You're more than any of those things to me. There won't be another Holly. Because there will never be another Connor Haus."

Connor moved away again, wanting Logan to stop. She couldn't say these things to her. They were too tempting. They sounded too good.

"I already told you, I don't want anything serious here." She forced her walls back up, but it was growing harder to keep Logan out. With every touch, every crooked grin, every dreamy squint from her magnetic blue eyes, Connor was losing control. And Logan was slowly, carefully, finding her way inside.

"I know what you told me. And I know what I told you. I'll wait for you."

"Don't say that," Connor argued, stoically.

"I'll wait for you. I will. I don't care if it takes you a decade. I'm not going anywhere. When you're ready, I'll be here."

A fleeting ambivalence pulsed through Connor. Why was she fighting this so hard? But it was quickly washed away by the memory of Logan, wrapping her hand around their patient's gun, wrestling him down like she was invincible. As good as wanting Logan felt in the moment, losing her would feel so much worse.

"Fine. Do what you want." But Connor couldn't help the shy smile she flashed Logan's way.

"I usually do." Logan smiled back at her, the smile that turned Connor's legs to useless puddles of mush, and took a bite of her taco. Suddenly, Connor couldn't get her out of there fast enough.

❖

"Chateau Curtis. Your wish is our command," Logan said, unlocking the door to her apartment and ushering Connor through. But Connor didn't go in just yet. Instead, she stopped at Logan and put her hands on her hips, reaching up to kiss her. She liked the way she had to balance on her toes, just a little, to get to her. She liked the way she fit in Logan's strong arms and the way she smelled when she rested her head against her chest. She liked the way she made her feel wanted and safe—even when she knew she shouldn't.

"Then this is my wish." Connor kissed her again, and let her hands wander up the back of her shirt, pulling it away from her pants.

"Let's go inside."

Connor couldn't help how much she wanted Logan. After three years of near celibacy, she was like a horny teenager who'd just learned how to make out. Besides, what was so wrong with having some casual sex? A lot of casual sex, actually. She was thirty-two years old and had been all but alone since Kam died. And now, this hard-bodied, equally hard-headed, smart, funny, compassionate woman wanted to take her to bed. How could she possibly resist? More importantly, why should she resist?

The last few times she'd been to Logan's apartment, Connor admittedly hadn't been looking at much else besides her. And for the first time, she noticed the baby grand piano sitting in the corner of the living room.

"Don't tell me you play," Connor said skeptically.

Logan grinned. "And what if I do?"

"Then I'd...well, I'd be very surprised. And impressed." She watched as Logan made her way to the piano, pulled out the bench, and sat down.

Without another word, Logan tickled a couple of keys, shrugged out of her jacket, and stretched her arms out in front of her. For several minutes, Connor watched and listened as Logan played a nearly perfect medley of Chopin and Bach. When Logan had finished, her hands visibly shaking just slightly, she turned and looked at Connor, who couldn't hide her awe.

"Logan..." Connor had actually forgotten how to form words. Somehow, Logan just kept surprising her. Surprising and impressing her. And she was making it incredibly difficult to keep her feelings in check.

Logan's cheeks were a subtle pink—something Connor was only used to seeing at a fire scene—and Connor made her way quietly to the piano and closed her arms around her waist.

"Just something I do in my free time," Logan said, her voice wavering with just a hint of insecurity.

"You are amazing." She leaned in and kissed Logan's neck, holding her tighter. Electricity pounded between them, and Connor felt her body nearly lift off the ground with a sense of anticipation and fear and rapture she hadn't felt in forever. God damn it. She was falling in love with her. This was the last thing she wanted. This was a death sentence.

Logan had gone as long as she could without having Connor. She knew she had to be more than just a good lay. But enough was enough. She was only human. She'd had three tacos, two beers, and played the piano for twenty-four minutes. They'd talked, and laughed, Logan keeping a safe distance between them in case she couldn't keep from touching her—which she knew she couldn't. Never in her life could she have imagined wanting anyone the way she wanted Connor. This wasn't even about falling in love with her anymore. No, she was already there. It was terrifying, like she knew it would be. But that fear couldn't stand up to the rush of Connor, in her arms, in her bed, in her heart.

As her thoughts wafted away, she realized she'd been staring at Connor, a big, sloppy smile on her face.

"What?" Connor asked, laughing.

"Huh?"

"Get over here." She grabbed Logan's hands and closed the several feet of space Logan had been keeping between them, pulling Logan's body on top of hers.

"You kill me," Logan mumbled, her lips just brushing Connor's.

"How do you mean?"

Logan sat up. "Here I am, trying to get to know you, and I mean really get to know you, and you won't stop throwing your panties at me."

Connor laughed again and playfully shoved her away.

"Oh, is that how it is? Am I harassing you, Firefighter Curtis?"

"Well..." Logan moved her hands to Connor's thighs. "Yes. How am I supposed to make you fall for me if I can't show you how excruciatingly, well, lovable I am?"

"Fall for you? Is that what you're trying to make me do?" Connor answered lightly, but her eyes were thick with worry. "And what makes you think I would do something like that?"

"I can only hope." Logan ran her hand through Connor's hair and kissed her, her tongue slowly tracing around Connor's lips until she felt her body shudder just slightly. She was great at turning women on. Logan only wished she was half as good at making them love her.

"I don't know about lovable," Connor said, tugging at Logan's earlobe with her teeth and scratching up her back, "but you are certainly excruciatingly sexy."

Something was lurking behind Connor's eyes. Something Logan could only interpret as fear. She wanted desperately to make it disappear with every touch. Making people feel safe was what Logan did for a living. It was her gift. So why couldn't she make Connor feel it? Logan eased her body on top of hers again, kissing Connor with all the skill and passion and allure she had in her, wanting more than anything to make her feel the way she did. She ran her fingers under Connor's dress, gently brushing the soft skin on the inside of her thighs, her muscles clenching at the sound of Connor's low, throaty moan. She traced her tongue down Connor's neck and nipped at her collarbone as she lifted the dress up and over her head.

"God, I want you," Connor whispered, pulling Logan's T-shirt off and running her palms up her hard stomach and over her breasts. "I wonder if I'll ever stop wanting you this much."

"Please don't."

Connor moved to Logan's belt and pulled at her pants, kissing her way down until she reached the band of her tight briefs.

"I don't think I could stop if I wanted to," she answered. The throbbing in Logan's heart mirrored the tension between her legs. Her vision blurred as Connor put her mouth to her again.

Too late, Logan told herself. I already love you.

## Chapter Sixteen

Connor didn't spend the night. When the afterglow of mind-blowing sex had begun to wear off, she was left with that old, unwavering urge to run. And sleeping next to Logan wouldn't help anything. Not when waking up next to her only magnified any and all feelings that she was quietly harboring, anyway. She didn't wait until the early morning this time, either, sneaking out while Logan slept.

As she left, Logan's sad eyes burning a hole straight through to her heart, she remembered her last night with Galen—*"We both know what this is, and what it isn't."* That was how it was *supposed* to be with Logan. But truth be told, neither of them had a clue what was happening between them. So Connor did the only thing she knew how to and walked away, desperate to fix the carnage and trauma of someone else's life. Because God knew she couldn't fix it in her own.

"You look like shit," Jake said plainly, as Connor entered the station the next morning.

"Laurie must just love being married to you."

"I'm not quite as frank with her. Do you think I'd still be married if I were?"

Connor laughed. "Nope."

"But really." Jake closed the ambulance doors and took a seat on the fender. "What happened to you last night? You look awful."

"Why are you here so early, anyway? It's only 6:20."

"Parker's teething. Poor little bugger's been crying all night. Which means Laurie doesn't sleep. Which means I don't sleep. I finally gave up at four a.m. and...Hey, wait. You're avoiding my question. Where were you?"

Connor didn't want to talk to Jake right now. She didn't want to tell him what she'd felt the night before had scared her so intensely, she couldn't explain it as anything but love. Jake would expect her to act. He would expect her to take accountability. And she just wasn't going to do that. No matter how she felt about Logan, she was still a disaster waiting to happen. She was like sleeping with wolves. Jake wouldn't understand.

"I was home."

"All night?"

"Yeah, all night." Connor exhaled loudly and shook her head. "Okay, no, not all night." She never could lie to Jake.

"Well, how did your date go then?"

"It was fine."

884's tone went out through the station, providing Connor with a rush of much-needed reprieve.

"Better go," she said, jumping into the front seat of the truck. Jake followed suit, and she knew she wasn't going to get out of this so easily.

"884 respond to Elmwood Assisted Living on Forsyth for a delta bravo seven. Eighty-four-year-old male, unresponsive. Over."

Connor picked up the mic, a familiar sense of confidence and relief spreading through her. She may have been incompetent when it came to her personal life, but she knew how to help people. If there was one thing she knew how to do, it was save a life. If only she could find that kind of confidence in everything else.

"884 responding, over."

Jake didn't speak during the entire seven minutes to the nursing home, and Connor knew he could fit a novel's worth of words into seven minutes. He was sure to be thinking, waiting for just the right moment to pounce and rip into her. Jake just wanted what was best for her. He just didn't realize how wrong he was yet.

"I love these calls," Connor said when she jumped out of the ambulance. The unresponsive patient was the ultimate mystery. It could be anything from low blood sugar to a stroke to an overdose, and you could easily miss the right diagnosis if you weren't paying attention. Or, if you weren't good. Luckily, Connor was good. She lived for solving these puzzles. Maybe if she were unresponsive, Connor thought as she walked into the nursing home, she could figure out what the hell was wrong with her.

"Tell me what happened."

A lone nurse whose English was poor at best stood at the patient's bedside.

"I found him like this," the nurse bit back coldly.

Connor looked at the man. His eyes were clouded over and his right pupil was sluggish and large. A trail of drool fell from the corner of his mouth, and his breathing was fast and shallow.

"Look at me, sir. Can you look at me?"

The man didn't respond.

"Can you smile for me? Come on, sir, give me a big smile."

The left side of his face curled into a weak smile, but the right side didn't move.

"He's having a stroke," Connor said to the nurse. "What's he on for meds?"

She looked at Connor blankly. "I don't know. My shift just started."

"Are you kidding me?" She turned to Jake, who was busy taking a blood pressure and putting oxygen on the man. "Jake, go find someone who knows something."

"I've got it." Logan's tall, strong frame appeared in the doorway of the man's tiny room, a piece of wrinkled paper in her perfect hands that Connor wanted so badly to be on her every minute of every hour of every goddamn day…

"What?" Connor looked up at her, confused, her heart skipping like a rock across water at the sound of her voice. She hadn't seen the engine when they pulled in.

"I've got his meds, his history, his family contacts… everything they have on him."

"Good." She allowed Logan the tiniest smile. Even in the midst of chaos, she was solid, unwavering. "You're riding with us, then. Let's go."

Logan's eyes widened a little, but she didn't argue. Everyone knew better than to argue with Connor on a scene—on her scene. Logan and Ace, who had appeared several minutes later from God only knew where, wheeled the man to the rig and lifted him inside. Jake blasted the sirens and pulled out of the parking lot while Connor started an IV.

"I thought no BFDs were allowed on board," Logan said with a wink.

"My rules. Therefore, I reserve the right to change them whenever I want." It was hard for even Connor to deny the chemistry between them. Their banter was thrilling and sexy, teetering somewhere between jesting and flirtation. Still, chemistry was just that—chemicals. It couldn't last. And it certainly couldn't protect anyone from loss.

"Okay, tell me what you've got," Connor added, adjusting the oxygen mask on the man's face.

"Walter Johnson. Eighty-four years old. History of type II diabetes, coronary artery disease, and a-fib. He's on metformin, lisinopril, fish oil and…Hold on, at the bottom here someone scribbled something in pencil. I can't really read it."

"Here, let me take a look." She squinted for a second at the faded, scrawling words, tensing her mouth and shaking her head. "Sonofabitch. It says Coumadin. It says 'started Coumadin on 3/15.' It's May now. I bet they haven't checked his levels in a month. He's bleeding into his brain."

"Pedal to the metal, Jake," Logan shouted to the front. "Hemorrhagic stroke."

Her body jerked back as the ambulance lunged forward. Connor was used to Jake's rodeoesque driving. She didn't budge.

"It's probably too late." Connor felt her face fall. Every time she lost someone, a very small piece of her died too, until she wondered just how much of her was left to lose. "If they'd only checked his fucking INR."

The ambulance came to an abrupt stop, and Jake came around and opened the back doors.

"What do you have?" Galen met them at the entrance of the ER, and Connor swore she saw her eyes twinkle when Logan jumped out of the back too.

"Walter Johnson, 84. Found this morning at a nursing home. He's aphasic and his right pupil is blown. Facial asymmetry. Just started on Coumadin in March. Looks like a hemorrhagic CVA." A sense of failure muffled the usual pep in Connor's voice.

"How long has he been like this?" Galen helped the others slide Walter into the ER bed.

"The nurse we talked to said she'd just started her shift. Probably all night though."

"Good work. I'm sending him right down for a head CT."

"Let me know how it turns out?" Connor asked, despondently.

"Of course." Galen reached out and squeezed her shoulder before rushing Walter off for testing. But not before Logan's eyes narrowed into a hard glare. Connor caught the jealousy and tension that drifted off Logan at Galen's touch. And the beat of arousal it sent through her was more than a little surprising.

"Thank you," Connor said, once she and Logan were alone outside of the trauma room.

"For what?"

"Showing up. Getting things done that no one else would." She smiled, glanced quickly down either end of the hall, and kissed her. "For being you."

Logan's lips burned and her face beat a hot red at the unexpected affection. And suddenly, Galen's little shoulder rub didn't seem quite so threatening.

"What are you doing tonight?" Logan asked, suddenly desperate for more. More of Connor's mouth. More of her voice. More of her everything.

"I have to pack. Jake and I are signed up for this wilderness EMT course tomorrow."

Logan couldn't believe her luck.

"In Maine?"

"Yeah. Out of Freeport. How did you know?"

"Because I'm in the same class."

Logan's heart battered the inside of her chest as she thought about five days in the woods with Connor. This was going to make any kind of learning more than a little challenging. And a lot more enjoyable.

"Stop it. It doesn't count if you run home right now and sign up."

"I swear." Logan laughed. "What do you take me for anyway? A stalker? Here, look." She took out her wallet and pulled out a folded piece of paper, handing it to Connor.

"Huh. Looks legit." Connor smiled playfully.

"Now will you apologize for calling me your stalker?"

"Fine. I'm sorry I called you such a name." She ran her hand softly up the inside of Logan's T-shirt sleeve. "I guess I'll see you at 0600 tomorrow then, Firefighter Curtis."

"Looking forward to it, Paramedic Haus."

Connor turned and walked away, and Logan collapsed against the wall, suddenly weak and unsteady.

❖

Connor was up before the sun, which wasn't unusual for her. But that morning was different. That morning she woke up to a grueling rumbling of anxiety in the depths of her stomach that was all but completely foreign to her. Absolutely nothing fazed Connor. Nothing, except for two things—the woods and Logan Curtis. And now, she'd be forced to face both.

She arrived at the nearly deserted parking lot of the designated shopping plaza where a rickety coach bus idled, waiting to take the group of EMTs and paramedics to the wilderness of Maine and leave them with nothing but a backpack filled with Luna bars and a pot-bellied ex-military lieutenant instructor who reeked of liquor. Connor wondered what she was thinking when she let Jake talk her into this. He knew Connor never backed down from a challenge. He also knew she hated bugs, and snakes, and cold, and sleeping on the ground. Hell, he probably also knew Logan would be there.

Halfway to the bus, she thought about turning around. No one was there to see. She could just get back on the subway and disappear, and avoid all of this. But before she did, she spotted Logan, resilient and graceful, stepping out of the early morning shadows. The unease that had been tumbling like an avalanche inside of her suddenly settled, and turning around was no longer an option.

"Who'd have thought you could look so cute with such an enormous pack on." Logan smiled and helped Connor take off her clearly excessive gear.

"Guess I overdid it a little, huh?"

"Kitchen sink and all?" Logan laughed and heaved the backpack underneath the bus.

"I've never done this kind of thing before. And if I'm being honest, I've kind of always been a bit of a city girl."

"Don't tell me you're afraid of bugs and dirt and peeing in bushes."

"I'm not afraid! I just don't particularly like any of those things. I like my warm, dry apartment, and my clean bathroom. Is that really so wrong?"

Logan stepped onto the bus ahead of her and took a seat in the back.

"So why are you doing this then? It's because I'm here, isn't it?"

Connor sat down beside her in the otherwise empty bus.

"You wish." She laughed and poked her side. "I'm here because Jake peer-pressured me into it. And you know how much I hate backing down from anything. Besides, I figure it might be good for me—a little time with nature."

"Don't worry." Logan stretched upward and put her arm tightly around Connor's shoulder. "I'll keep you safe."

"My hero." Connor stuck out her tongue and forced a gag.

"Hot damn," Jake said, walking onto the bus and heading quickly toward them.

"Hey, Jake." Connor waited.

"Logan, I had no idea you were coming on this little hike with us." He smiled devilishly. "Well, I think it's safe to say things just got interesting. Am I right?"

Before Connor could answer, Marty Taylor, Ace, and one of their other BFD brothers boarded, laughing and shoving each other.

"Who invited Delta Kappa Dumb?" Connor said, teasing them.

"You should be so lucky to have me out there in the woods with you, Haus," Taylor answered. "It gets awful cold at night, you know. Someone has to keep you warm." He grinned and reached out to touch Connor's face, but she slapped his hand away before he got anywhere close.

"Don't be a creep, Taylor," she answered.

"I'm just playing. You know that."

"Yeah, well, it's not funny," Logan growled.

"Down, Logan." He turned back to Connor. "I see you already have someone to share your sleeping bag with."

"That's enough, Marty," Jake said, gesturing for him to sit down. Connor knew, they all knew, actually, that Taylor still hurt over Kam every day. That was no excuse to take things one step too far, but on some level, Connor understood. She'd been there too.

A few hours later, the bus pulled onto a dirt road that dead-ended at a rusty gate surrounded by overgrown weeds and vines. Through the trees a narrow trail was barely evident. Connor's stomach turned.

"You okay?" Logan whispered as they walked out.

"Oh yeah. Fine. Why?"

"You look a little pale. Beautiful, but pale."

Connor smiled, hoping Logan's charm and calming presence would be enough to get her through the next several days.

"I'll be okay." She grabbed Logan's arm, wishing she could hold onto her for the remainder of the day. But she knew she had to be careful. Letting her affections be on display on a work outing was one thing, but doing it in front of Jake, Taylor, and his goons was something else completely.

"Everyone listen up." The short, stout man in the faded military fatigues stood in front of them, looking slightly bored. "We're going to hike five miles out and set up camp there. That'll be it for the day. Then we'll start first thing tomorrow with a quick lesson on extrication and some rope work. Hope you're all ready for this. I don't have time for anyone to get sick or hurt or piss their pants out there. Let's go."

Just before dusk, their group of six made their way into the clearing that marked the end of the long hike, with Connor and Logan heading the pack and Jake trailing from behind. As she unbuckled the straps of her pack and tossed it gratefully into the dirt, Connor caught a long, tempting glance of Logan. Her damp gray T-shirt clung to her back, and pieces of her thick hair fell out from under her baseball cap and kissed her shoulders. Streaks of dirt smudged her bare legs and cheek, and Connor's fatigue suddenly dissipated, replaced by a carnal need to pull the sweat-stained shirt from her body.

"How about helping me with my tent?" Connor asked, bashfully, grateful for what was surely a fresh sunburn to cover the red in her face.

"Of course."

Logan unpacked the tent from Connor's backpack and began laying out the nylon and putting stakes in the ground. In just a few short minutes, she had it standing, Connor's sleeping bag spread out perfectly inside.

"And by help me, I apparently meant, can you set up my tent for me?"

"Hey, look. I've been at this for a long time. You're good at plenty of things that I'm not. Just let me help."

Connor looked at the ground and smiled, her need for Logan only building by the minute. "Yeah, well, thank you."

"Haus! Logan! Time for hot dogs!" Jake was poking at the campfire while Taylor and Ace arm-wrestled on a nearby rock. Their crusty instructor was nowhere in the vicinity.

"I don't know about this guy," Connor said as they warmed their dinner over the hot coals.

"Who?" Logan asked.

"Our instructor. He hasn't exactly given us much in the way of, you know, instruction. And he seems sort of drunk most of the time."

"You're just being paranoid," Jake said.

"Jake, you of all people should know what a good judge of character I am. It doesn't take me more than a few minutes to figure someone out completely."

Jake looked at Logan, raised his eyebrows, and then looked at Connor. "Oh, is that right?"

"Yeah, it is."

"I don't think you're always right about *everyone*." He shook his head Logan's way, and Logan let out a shout of laughter.

"You're right. I'm sure he's fine," Connor added, desperate to change the direction of the conversation.

The sky was dark now, and Connor had to admit, the stars were unlike anything she could possibly see from Boston. The instructor stumbled out of his tent, clutching a water bottle half full of something that was definitely not water.

"We have a long day tomorrow. Everyone should turn in. I expect quiet for the rest of the night. No shenanigans."

Connor eyed the others nervously and stood up. "I'm exhausted anyway. I'm going to bed. Good night, guys."

She stopped for just a second to look at Logan, her eyes projecting the heat that had been building in her all day.

"Yeah. I'm going too. Good night." Logan followed and unzipped her tent that was only a few feet from Connor's. Connor wished more than anything that she didn't have to go to bed alone.

"Fine. But for the record I think you guys are a bunch of party poopers," Taylor said.

"Party poopers, Taylor?" Connor called from her tent. "What are you, ten?"

"Ten inches, maybe." He laughed hard at himself.

"You're gross. Now everyone shut up and get to sleep."

Connor knew it was early. And she knew the boys would have rather stayed up making themselves sick on marshmallows and swapping stories about breasts. But she was also sure that if she listened to the instructor, the others would have to follow suit. The sooner everyone went to sleep, the sooner she could see Logan again.

## CHAPTER SEVENTEEN

Connor lay there in the dark for an hour, waiting for the muffled giggles coming from the boys' tents to fade to silence. When they finally did, she unzipped her tent just enough to slip through, walked the few steps to Logan's, and opened the flap. Logan was asleep, the sound of her quiet breathing Connor was growing to love so much coming softly from her parted lips. She spotted the open zipper of her sleeping bag and crawled in, cradling herself against Logan and kissing her neck. Logan's skin was soft and salty, and the taste of her sent a jolt that ripped straight through Connor.

"I thought we were told no shenanigans," Logan whispered, her eyes still closed and her lips curling into a sweet smile.

"I thought you knew I wasn't a very good listener."

"What was I thinking?"

"Shhh." Connor kissed her mouth, sliding her tongue past Logan's full lips. She pulled back just enough. "I'll be pissed if you wake them up before I get to have you at least twice."

Logan ran her hand under Connor's thin cotton T-shirt and cupped her breasts, brushing a thumb over her already hard nipples. She kissed her again, gently biting her lower lip and sucking it into her own mouth. Her fingers trailed lightly down Connor's stomach and landed at the waist of her long johns, where she tucked her hand inside and continued her soft, teasing touches until Connor was chewing on her own tongue to keep quiet, her legs writhing, her breath wild.

❖

"Wake up, lovebirds," Jake said quietly from outside Logan's tent.

Connor didn't remember falling asleep. And she certainly didn't remember falling asleep with Logan. Damn it.

"Jake."

Connor jumped out of Logan's arms and out of the tent, quietly thanking God she seemed to have all her clothes on.

"Relax. I'm the only one up so far. I went to take you coffee this morning and saw your tent was empty."

"How'd you know I was here?"

"Really?" Jake asked, sounding incredulous.

"Point taken. Thank you, though. I don't know what I would have done if Taylor had found me in there this morning. I'd never hear the end of it."

"No, you definitely wouldn't. You owe me."

She patted Jake on the back and they walked off toward the now-doused campfire.

By the time Taylor, Ace, and Logan got up, Jake and Connor already had a new fire going and were boiling stream water for the day and mixing together something Connor could only call oatmeal. Their instructor followed next, his eyes rimmed as red as his nose. Connor knew what alcoholics looked like. She'd taken care of plenty of them. She had no doubt this guy clung to the bottle still. She only hoped his habit wouldn't cost them their lives out there.

"Enough slop. Pack it up and move it down by the river. We'll start with rope work in fifteen minutes."

They did as they were told, but Connor couldn't help but notice the menacing shade of gray the sky had taken on.

"I didn't think it was supposed to rain this week," she mentioned to Logan as they hiked the mile up trail to the river.

"Probably just a shower."

❖

Jake was about a minute from being lowered into the still-icy river when the clouds opened up and a cold, heavy rain pummeled them from overhead. The storm came so hard, and so fast, they hardly had time to move. Trees were bending to their breaking point in the fierce winds, and a crack of thunder came from just above them.

"Everybody take cover," the instructor barked. "See that set of boulders at three o'clock. That'll work. Go."

They ran down the stream to the cluster of enormous rocks that offered shelter from the hail now shooting from the sky. Logan took Connor's hand and pulled her into the opening of a small cave, her drenched clothes now glued to her skin.

"You okay?" she asked Connor.

"Yeah, I'm fine." Connor shook from the cold, welcoming Logan's warm arms around her.

Jake and the others appeared a minute later, the instructor lagging behind. Connor watched him take a pull from a small flask before crouching into the shelter.

"This'll pass," the instructor muttered. "We'll just wait it out here."

But the storm didn't pass. At least not quickly. They remained huddled under the safety of the boulders while the hail that had pounded the outside world shifted to an unrelenting, heavy rain. Connor had stopped shivering, but she worried about what kind of damage had already been done. Still, the security of Logan's arms around her lightened the burden.

"Anyone have a deck of cards and some vodka?" Taylor said.

"What about our stuff?" Jake asked. "Everything was outside."

Connor thought that was a great question and looked to the instructor for answers. But he had none. His face was ashen and a fine sheen had covered his forehead. Connor knew enough to realize when someone didn't look good, and he definitely didn't look well.

"Are you all right?" Connor asked him.

"I'll be fine. Just don't feel up to snuff. Probably those hot dogs last night." The instructor reached up and massaged the center of his chest, wincing.

"Are you having chest pain?"

"I was an army corpsman for thirty-four years. I'd know if something wasn't right," he snarled.

Connor backed down, but the alarms in her gut were screaming.

An hour later, the rain that hammered against the rocks settled to a quiet patter, and they ventured away from the shelter. The river had risen nearly to the banks in the wake of what must have been a flash flood, and trees had been stripped of their leaves. They were able to make the mile hike back to base, but fallen branches and newly formed lake-sized puddles made their trek treacherous and difficult at best. When they crossed into the clearing, Connor gasped. The campsite had been washed away, replaced by inches of mud and destruction.

"Our gear…" Jake said.

Everyone except the instructor ran to where their tents and packs and fire had been. It was gone, nearly all of it. And what wasn't gone was useless. Logan wandered off and returned with her gear, which Connor had noticed she'd secured to a tree with a piece of strong rope under the haven of some heavy-hanging bows. She was the only one who knew to stow her things in case of bad weather, or bears, or whatever else found its way to them.

"Mine looks okay," she said.

"Well, good for you," Taylor grumbled. He turned to the instructor, who had grown paler and propped himself against a tree. "What do we do now?"

"We…" Before he could get out another word, his eyes rolled into the back of his head, and he collapsed to the ground.

"Haus! Sergeant Douchebag passed out. Get over here."

Connor rushed to his side, dropping to her knees and placing her ear over his mouth.

"He's breathing." She picked up his wrist and felt for a pulse—it was weak and erratic. "But I think he's having an MI. I've been watching him. He's been looking like hell all day. We have to turn back. He needs help."

"How?" Jake asked. "The guy has to weigh at least 250 pounds. And it's five miles to base."

Logan came out from behind a clearing carrying a backboard covered in mud and several arm-lengths of rope.

"We're going to carry him," she said, confidently. "Taylor, Jake, get over here and help me."

Connor looked up at Logan, her heart swelling in her chest, and she couldn't think of anyone she'd rather have with her in the middle of hell.

"Cut this into four equal pieces," Logan ordered Taylor, handing him the rope and a pocketknife. "Jake, help Connor lay him down. Be careful. He may have hit his head on the way."

Everyone listened quietly, Logan's sense of power and poise palpable. When the instructor was flat on the ground, Connor, Jake, and Logan slid him onto the backboard, and Logan tied the rope around his legs, his middle, and his chest until he was secure. She took four more pieces of rope and tied two to either end of the board.

"Taylor, Connor, you guys take the back. Jake and I will get his head."

"Oh, you've got to be kidding me," Taylor said in a whine.

"Marty, he's going to die. Get your shit in order, will you?" Jake barked.

Connor and Logan exchanged pleased glances, and all four of them picked up the ropes and lifted the instructor into the air, while Ace and the other BFD grabbed what was left of Logan's gear.

❖

"I don't know how much longer I can do this," Jake said. They'd made it two miles out, and his arms were visibly shaking under the tension of carrying the heavy load down the mountain.

"You may not have to…" Logan said.

The caravan came to a halt.

"What is it? Why are we stopping?" Connor asked from the back.

"That's why. Lower him to the ground." Everyone did as they were told, and when the instructor's massive frame was out of the way, the view of the washed-out trail was suddenly as clear as the now-blue sky above them.

"Fuck." Connor didn't know much about hiking, but she knew that a blocked path couldn't be good. A boulder nearly the size of the ones that had seen them through the storm stood directly in their way. And it wasn't going anywhere.

"Can't we just go around it?" Jake asked.

"We can't." Logan bowed her head to the ground. "Look down the trail farther."

"I can't see anything," he said.

"That's because there's nothing there. It's gone. The trail is gone."

Everyone was quiet again. A small gurgling sound came from the instructor's mouth, and his eyes shot open, wide and frightened.

"Sir, you're awake," Connor said, checking his pulse again.

"What…happened…" he said weakly.

"We think you're having a heart attack. We're trying to take you back down to get help, but the trail is gone."

He tried to sit up, but the ropes still held him tightly.

"Try…radio…" he whispered, and his eyes fluttered closed again.

"Fuck me! The radio!" Jake shouted. "Why the hell didn't we think of that?"

"We did," Logan said. "I tried it before we left. It's out too. Apparently Mr. Survival here didn't think to stow his gear either."

"So what do we do?" Taylor asked.

Connor watched as Logan's brow deepened. She seemed to have an answer for everything. And Connor had never felt safer than she did in that moment.

"Cell phone. Does anyone have a cell phone?" Logan finally said.

"He said no cell phones, remember? We all left them back in the bus," Jake answered.

"I didn't," Taylor said quietly.

"Taylor, you jackass. You've had a cell phone this entire time and you didn't tell us?" Logan barked.

"I didn't think of it! I'm sorry! Here." He reached into his cargo pocket and pulled out his phone, tapping hard on the screen. "Shit. Battery's dead."

"Of course it is," Jake said.

All six began talking at once, no one to anyone in particular, until a steady hum of voices had built up echoes into the mountains.

"All right, everyone listen up," Logan yelled. Everyone stopped. "I studied the map of these trails for a week before we left. This is our only way down. We have to make camp here and try to signal for help. I have four protein bars, six iodine tablets, and a bag of trail mix. I don't know how long we'll be here, but I do know that's not going to be enough."

Connor's legs nearly buckled, and she wasn't sure whether it was the hike or the command in Logan's voice.

"Jake, Ace, go look for food. Anything that we can cook, we can eat. Stay away from berries. Your best bet is to look near the water. Snakes, rodents, I don't care. We may need it. Fish are ideal. But we can't be picky right now. Connor, you'll stay here with me and help me find wood for a signal fire. Everyone else, keep trying that radio and watch him. You're both EMTs. If he codes, do CPR. Whatever you do, everyone stay together. And be back here in two hours."

No one argued. They all went to work, while Connor stayed at Logan's side.

"Come on," Logan said. Connor had never seen her so focused and strong, even on scene. She followed without question around the perimeter of the new campsite, helping Logan collect pieces of brush and leaves. Neither of them spoke.

"Are we going to be okay?" Connor asked, suddenly frightened. Logan stopped and faced her, wrapping her arms around her like a blanket until Connor was warm and comforted.

"Of course we are. I promise. I'll get us out of here. I told you…I'll save you."

Connor looked up at her and smiled, holding onto her tightly. "My hero."

## Chapter Eighteen

By nightfall, Logan and Connor had a whopping fire going, and Jake and Ace had come back with one small fish, a frog, and a handful of insects that made Connor's stomach turn.

"Any luck with the radio?" Logan asked Taylor.

"Nothing."

"How's he doing?" she asked, pointing to the instructor's nearly lifeless body.

"You know, not great. Still alive, for now. But not good," Taylor answered.

Logan nodded quietly. "We need to put up a shelter for the night." She moved to her pack and unfolded a thirty-foot tarp, spreading it on the ground.

"What are we going to do with that?" Jake asked.

"Anyone good at climbing trees?"

"I'm all right," Jake said, a sly grin materializing on his face.

"Good. Take this corner and climb up about fifteen feet with it. Then tie it as tight as you can. Do the same thing with the other three corners on those trees over there."

Jake shook his head eagerly and started up the first tree.

In about forty-five minutes, Logan had a large-enough shelter to fit all seven of them, with a bed of brush and grass lining the ground like a lumpy mattress.

"I'll take the first shift," Logan said. "Someone needs to stay up with him. You guys should get some rest."

"I'm staying with you." Connor came up behind her and put her arms around her, squeezing her tightly.

"You need to sleep."

"I'll sleep later. I want to be with you."

Logan couldn't protest too much. Not when Connor looked so vulnerable and scared. Not when she made even two days' worth of dirt and sweat and muddy T-shirts look painfully appealing. When she'd heard Connor would be on this trip with her, she'd had delusions of making her fall in love. Now, she only hoped she could get her out of here alive.

"You really were my hero today, you know," Connor said. She sat next to Logan in front of the dancing fire. Connor seemed content just to be there with her, and Logan's heart stirred. She smiled at Connor, overwhelmed with fatigue and worried, but unable to shake the unyielding hope that Connor's presence always brought. Connor nestled up against her and let her head fall onto Logan's shoulder.

"It was nothing."

"Don't start being humble on me now," Connor said, teasing her.

"Why, Connor?" Logan did her best to keep her voice steady. "Why what?"

"Why are you fighting this?"

Connor looked at her, obviously perplexed. "Excuse me?"

"Us. God, you're clueless." She let her forehead drop into her hands.

"That's what Jake always says."

"You don't get it, do you? I'm in love with you, Connor. I've never been in love with anyone before. In fact, I don't even think I've really ever liked anyone before. But here it is. I'm in love with you. And I think, if you'll just admit it to yourself, you're in love with me too."

"Logan I…" Connor turned away from her. Logan waited, hoping with every inch of her that Connor would return the words that made her feel like she was walking naked into a burning building. "I'm going to go."

"Go where? We're stranded in the middle of nowhere."

"I'm going to sleep," Connor answered coldly. Before Logan could think of anything clever to get her to stay, she was gone.

❖

Logan sat alone on the tree stump by the fire for several more hours, her heart aching like it never had before. They were stranded in the woods with only a few meal bars, a dead fish the size of her hand, and a couple more bottles of clean water. But she couldn't care about anything other than Connor walking away. She'd never told anyone she loved them before. And she definitely hadn't known what it felt like not to hear it back.

"Hey, mind if I sit out here for a while?" Jake came up from behind her and put a comforting hand on her shoulder.

"Sure, why not? Pull up a tree."

He sat on a rock beside her and just looked at Logan for a long time.

"What happened?" he asked.

"The trail got washed out. What do you mean?"

"Not with the trail. With Connor. She came back into the shelter hours ago, didn't say a word, and then let out some of those little sniffles she does when she doesn't want anyone to know she's crying."

Logan hadn't realized how well Jake really knew Connor.

"I told her I loved her," Logan said, timid and embarrassed.

"And now she's crying. Makes sense," Jake said.

"It does?"

"Sure it does. Connor doesn't want to love you, Logan. Although, just between us, I'm pretty sure she does anyway."

"She does?" Logan nearly jumped out of her seat, a ray of hope penetrating her like the first spring sunlight.

"Yes. And I wish that were enough for her. But she's just too scared."

Logan looked into the darkness. "Tell me about Kam."

"Kam? Why?"

"Just tell me about her. What was she like? What was she like with Connor?"

Jake looked at her for a while, his face twisted in confusion. Logan wasn't sure why she needed to know Kam, but it suddenly seemed like the most important thing in the world.

"She was kind. And funny. She was rarely serious, actually. Which always kept things interesting, because we all know how serious Connor is. I don't think she really believed she could die. And that's why she did."

"She really loved Connor?" Logan asked.

"More than anything. They had that stupid, movie kind of love. You know, they couldn't keep their hands off each other. Made everyone want to barf all the time."

Logan's stomach twisted. "And Connor really loved her."

"It nearly killed her when Kam died. In fact, I think in a way, it did. But that's all changed since she met you. It's like she's come back to life."

"I wish Connor could see that," Logan answered, sadly.

"Me too."

"Thanks, Jake. Listen, do you mind checking on the instructor for me? Just make sure he's hanging in there? Not much else we can do for him out here."

"Yeah. No problem."

Jake left, and Logan let herself cry for the first time she could remember.

❖

Logan opened her eyes the next morning to a blinding sunlight, the sound of unfamiliar voices coming from nearby.

"Are you guys okay?" one of the voices called.

Logan cleared the grogginess from her head and tried to make sense of the words. She hadn't remembered falling asleep but found herself leaning against the stump she'd been sitting on with her raincoat around her legs.

"Over here!" the voice called again. It was closer this time. Two hikers, a man and a woman, looking better than the six in Logan's group, approached the camp where the signal fire was finally beginning to fade away. "Are you all all right?"

"No. We're stuck here," Logan answered. "The trail's all wiped out. And our survival guide had a heart attack yesterday. We need to get him down."

"We have a radio," the man next to her answered.

"Oh, thank God."

"I'll call the ranger station." The woman went off in search of a clear signal, and Logan exhaled deeply.

"What's going on?" Jake asked, emerging from the shelter bleary eyed.

"We've got help. They have a radio!"

"Oh my God. I was starting to think I'd never see Parker again."

"Come on. You knew we'd get out of here," Logan assured him.

"I guess I did. I just didn't know how long we'd be stuck in this hell hole."

Connor and the others came out next.

"We're rescued?!" Connor shouted.

"They're radioing for help right now," Logan said.

Connor moved toward Logan eagerly, as if to put her arms around her, and then stopped abruptly and looked down at the ground. The pain from the night before resurfaced violently for Logan.

"Okay, they're sending a helicopter," the woman said, once she'd returned with the radio.

"Yes!" Jake hugged Connor tightly and Logan watched them, an excruciating sadness nearly choking her.

By the time they made it back to the bus, Logan still hadn't spoken to Connor. She looked despondent and aloof, and it was making Connor crazy. Why did Logan have to go ahead and say she loved her anyway? Now everything was a mess.

"Come back to my place," Connor whispered to Logan, who now sat in the seat behind her on the way home.

"I don't think so."

"Why not?"

"We just got off the mountain," Logan answered, coldly.

"So? Come with me. I need you."

"What for? You want a quick fuck? No thanks. I'm good."

Connor's heart sank. She'd never seen this side of Logan. And she couldn't help but wonder if she'd made a massive mistake. No, she hadn't. Logan was right to say Connor was falling for her. She felt it too. But she just couldn't give herself over to her. She couldn't give herself over to love.

"Just to talk. Please?" Connor pleaded.

"We can talk when we get back. But I'm not coming over."

Logan spent the remainder of the ride trying to convince herself to let Connor go. She saw no point in holding on anymore. It was clear now that the hole that had been cut into Connor when Kam died was far from healed. And she would never be able to fill that void. Connor was waiting for her when she got off the bus.

"Why won't you come with me?" Connor lightly brushed her hand against Logan's chest. "We've had a horrible couple of days. Let me cook you the best dinner you've ever had. Then we can curl up on the couch with a bottle of wine and enjoy being warm and full again."

"Thanks, but I'll pass." Logan turned away sharply.

"What did I do?"

"Nothing. You didn't do anything."

Connor took her by the shoulders and spun her back around. "Then what is the matter with you? Turning down an invitation for a hot meal and a night of passionate, no-strings sex?"

"That's exactly it, Connor. I want strings."

"I already told you I—"

"I know what you told me. And now it's my turn to tell you." Logan shook her head hard. "God, I've been so stupid. I can't believe it took me so long to see."

"See what?" Connor was suddenly sick at the thought of never being able to touch Logan again.

"You aren't ready. You aren't going to love me until you can move on from Kam. She's gone, Connor. And that really sucks. Believe me, I can't begin to tell you how much I wish every goddamn day that I could take away the pain I see in your eyes. But I can't. No one can bring her back. But you're alive. And so am I. And I can't be the only one that sees that anymore."

Connor didn't speak. She tried to keep her expression cold and detached, but her heart crumbled at another good-bye. It seemed like her life had been nothing but good-byes lately. No one was dead. But somehow, Logan's good-bye felt almost as permanent and just as suffocating.

"So you're ending it."

"Yes. I'm ending it. It took me a long time to fall in love with someone. And I'm not going to waste my feelings on a girl who isn't ready to love me back."

"That's ridiculous and selfish!" Connor shook with anger. She'd known Logan would walk away—that is, if she didn't get herself killed first.

"Maybe. But I can't compete with your memories anymore. Good-bye, Connor."

# CHAPTER NINETEEN

Logan wasn't a crier. She was tough and stubborn. She was a firefighter. So she didn't make a habit of breaking down, no matter how desolate things seemed. But she barely made it off the subway that night before thick, wet tears spilled down her dirt-smeared cheeks. By the time she reached the steps of her apartment, she'd managed to pull herself together, the stinging in her eyes a painful reminder that something wasn't right. The world was off its axis. This wasn't how it was supposed to be. This wasn't how it was supposed to end for them.

Annie greeted her at the door. "What are you doing home?"

"Long story."

"Are you okay?" Logan's sister knew her well enough to know she was not okay. Asking was nothing more than a formality.

"Yes and no." She picked up the heavy pack and stowed it in the hall closet. "I'm going to shower."

"Wait. What happened out there?"

Logan sighed, not sure if even she could answer that question. "Just give me a minute, all right?" Annie nodded and Logan retreated to the bathroom, stripped out of her clothes, and thought about what her day would look like now that Connor was no longer in it.

❖

Annie was waiting for her when she got out, a glass of whiskey and a plate of crab Rangoons on the table in front of her.

"You look awful. Here, eat." She pushed the plate toward Logan.

"Thanks, but I'm not hungry." Logan picked up the whiskey and downed it in one hard gulp.

"Talk."

Logan got up from the couch, poured herself another two fingers, and sat back down. "There was a storm while we were out there," she said, matter-of-factly. "It wiped out the trail, and we were stuck on the mountain for the night."

"What? Logan! Are you all okay?"

"We're fine. Or, sort of..." Logan closed her eyes and saw Connor wrapping her arms around her in front of the signal fire.

"What do you mean 'sort of'?"

"Our instructor had a heart attack while we were hiking. But he's going to make it. That's all."

"What a mess. But why do I get the feeling that's not all?" Annie asked.

"I don't know."

"You've been crying."

Logan reached up and rubbed her eyes. "No."

"Don't insult me. I know you. And I don't think I've seen you cry since you were ten and Dad ran over your bike."

Logan laughed unexpectedly, until the laughter escalated into quiet sobs.

"Oh, Loge...what happened?" Annie grabbed her shirt, pulled her into her, and cradled her like a child.

"I love her," she finally said through stifled cries.

"I know you do." Annie rubbed soothing circles on her back as Logan sniffed.

"She's never going to be able to feel the same."

"How can you be so sure?"

Logan sat up and blinked hard. "She won't let herself. She's in love with a ghost."

"I'm so sorry."

"You know," Logan said, "all this time I thought I was broken. I thought I was just too fucked up to fall in love. Now, I only wish that were true."

❖

For the first time in a decade, Connor was dreading going into work. God, who was she if she couldn't even enjoy her job anymore? The thought of saving people was lacking its usual jolt of exhilaration. And the thought of seeing Logan again was downright appalling. Still, she got up that morning at five a.m., showered, fed Rusty, and put on her uniform. She had followed this same routine for years, but it had never felt mundane until today.

Three days had passed since they'd left the woods, and her life had been eerily quiet. Not peaceful, but quiet. Connor was quick to note the difference. She missed Logan in a way that was alarmingly close to death. Without Kam, she'd lost her footing, her purpose. But she hadn't realized just how much she'd regained it by loving Logan. And now, she was slipping again, tenacity and a relative indifference to anything other than work replacing the joy. In some ways, this was so much worse than losing Kam. Logan was still here. There had been no fire. Connor was choosing to walk away.

❖

Connor had miraculously managed to spend the first half of her shift dodging Logan like a bad case of the flu. The morning had been unnervingly calm, and at the few calls she did go on, Logan's engine company was nowhere to be found. Every time

Jake pulled the rig on scene and Logan wasn't there, she breathed a sigh of sweet relief. But that relief quickly gave way to the choking sense of loss and a deep-dwelling panic. How could she ever convince herself she'd done the right thing?

"I'm going to swing into BMC. I want to grab a sandwich from the EMS room," Jake said. They'd been driving around Boston more or less aimlessly, waiting for someone to get hurt or sick or even need help getting out of their recliner. At this point, Connor would settle for anything.

"Those sandwiches are gross."

"Yeah, but they're also free. Do you have any idea how much diapers cost?"

Connor glared at him.

"No, Jake. I don't. Why would I? It's not like I have a child. It's not like I have a partner. Or even a girlfriend for that matter. It's not like I have anyone other than you and Rusty."

"Whoa." Jake held up a hand. "Sorry, Princess Cranky. You're touchy today. Even for you."

"Sorry." Connor lowered her head, feeling guilty for taking her frustration and hurt out on the one person in the world who always had her back. Jake wasn't going anywhere. Jake wouldn't get himself killed. It wasn't his fault Logan was reckless.

"I'll just be a minute." Jake turned the ambulance into the Boston City ER parking lot and cut the brake. "Want anything?"

"I'll go with you. Better than sitting here bathing in my own self-pity." But Connor couldn't help but notice the part of her that quietly hoped Logan was nearby.

Connor trailed behind Jake, nervously eyeing every corner of the hospital they passed, torn between a terrifying need to hide and an equally disturbing need to set eyes on Logan again.

"Hurry up and let's go," she said, nudging Jake. Suddenly, she had to get out of there. The EMS room was far too small, and she instantly felt suffocated and stifled. Jake took his time shuffling through the sandwiches in the tiny refrigerator while Connor's panic escalated.

This time, she didn't even need to smell Logan's fiery, inviting scent. She could just feel her. Her body tingled and her mind raced. Somehow, she knew Logan was right behind her.

Jake stood, satisfied, with an armful of food. His gaze fixed behind Connor. "Crap."

"Let's go, Jake." Connor couldn't manage to turn around. Turning around meant facing Logan. It meant facing what was quite possibly the most horrendous error of her life. She contemplated walking backward out of the room. But, thinking that tripping on herself might only exacerbate the situation, she decided against it. She couldn't help but catch Logan's cold eyes as she passed. The usually soft, shining blue of her irises had melted into a pool of hurt and loss. It was the kind of loss Connor knew all too well because she knew her eyes reflected the same pain.

"Sorry about that," Jake mumbled once they'd reached the hall. "I didn't know she'd be here." But Connor was still staring at Logan.

"Huh?"

"Never mind. Let's just get out of here." Jake tugged her arm.

"Not yet." Connor wanted to go. She wanted to stop the hemorrhaging. But she couldn't move. She continued to watch like she was caught up in a nightmare, or a movie, as Logan's scowl softened into a coy smile, and she slid her chair close to one of the ER nurses they all knew. They knew her because she'd been seen with Galen Burgess more than once. And the rumors that she was more than a little hot for that breed of first responders was proving a little too true as she reached up and played with a strand of Logan's hair. Connor couldn't make out what was said. She wasn't even sure if she wanted to. But it didn't take words to figure out what was being said between the two. So this was how it was going to be. In a matter of days, this woman who had been "head over heels in love" was already looking to bed someone else.

"Seriously, Connor. You're making this awkward," Jake said. But Connor didn't care. Standing outside the door of the EMS room, watching Logan flirt unapologetically with the bouncy redheaded nurse, sent her heart into a tailspin. And before she could bring herself to think about what she was doing, Connor had burst back into the room.

"Do words mean anything to you?"

Logan stood up, apparently stunned to silence.

"Answer me, Logan. All that bullshit about being in love with me, is that what it was? Bullshit?"

"Connor. You're making a scene," Logan said quietly.

"No more of a scene than you're making in here with Nurse Sleeps-Around."

The redhead next to Logan stood up next, her brow diving deep into her forehead. "Excuse me? You don't even know me. And for the record, I am very seriously involved with Dr. Burgess."

Jake couldn't seem to help but let out a loud laugh from outside the door. And at that, the nurse had had enough. She stormed off, leaving Logan and Connor alone together.

"What are you doing?" Logan said, incredulously. Suddenly, Connor wasn't so sure. All at once, her sanity had taken flight and was nothing more than a fond, safe memory.

"Nothing. I have to go."

Logan grabbed her elbow. "You have to go? After all that, you have to go?"

"What do you want me to say, Logan?"

"You can start with why you just went off the handle on Melissa."

"Melissa? Is that her name? Well, clearly you two have gotten close," Connor said snidely.

"Not really, no. If you care, which, it's pretty clear you do, I see her now and then when I bring patients in. You'd probably know her too if you paid a little more attention."

"Don't turn this around on me."

"You barged in here. You must have something to say to me. So what is it?" Logan kept her voice low, but Connor could see her eyes were screaming. Connor stood, humiliated, feeling completely out of control emotionally.

"You're right. I have nothing to say to you." But she did. She had so much to say to her. Connor just couldn't find the words, or the courage. "Good-bye, Logan." She turned to go.

"Connor," Logan called after her. "How many more times are you going to make me say good-bye?"

## CHAPTER TWENTY

Logan Curtis had become the Ice Queen now. And it was completely, irrevocably, Connor's fault. Still, it was better this way. As long as Logan hated her, she would keep her distance. And as long as she kept her distance, Connor stood a chance at hanging onto her heart. She flinched at the memory of pain and anger in Logan's eyes earlier that day. And the way her stomach knotted inside of her made her think maybe she hadn't done such a good job hanging onto her heart after all. Visceral reactions aside, Logan had been right. She wasn't ready. Losing Kam had beaten and jaded her. She had nothing left to give.

"Oh, for fuck's sake." Jake punched Connor's shoulder from the driver's seat.

"Ow! That really hurt!"

"Good! At least now you have something to sulk about."

"What are you talking about?"

"This whole angsty teenager routine. I have zero sympathy for you."

Connor turned away, embarrassed. "Fine."

"And don't you want to know why?" Jake tapped his fingers on the steering wheel.

"Sure." She sighed. "Why, Jake?"

"You blew it, Haus. You had Logan. She was crazy about you. You were the one to come in and change her entire world. Do you have any idea how big of a deal that is?"

Connor just looked at him blankly.

"No, of course you don't. You know why? Because you're dense. No. That's too nice. You're more than dense. You're... you're an idiot! But you know what gets me more than anything? You love her."

"I don't love her." Connor couldn't keep herself from stuttering.

"You do. And you haven't loved anyone since Kam. Now *that's* a big fucking deal."

"You don't know what you're talking about." Connor's voice was flat in spite of the tornado of feelings that coiled inside of her.

"Oh, but I do. No one knows you better than I do, Haus. You're in love with her. And I'll keep saying it until you stop looking so terrified. You love her, and you fucked up. She's gone."

Connor's heart dropped and her eyes suddenly blurred.

"What do you mean, gone?"

"I mean..." Jake sighed. "Taylor told me today that she put in for a transfer back to Chicago."

"What?" Boiling-hot tears overwhelmed the burning in her eyes. "Oh. Well, good for her then. I hope she's happy there."

"You do, huh?" Jake reached over and took her in his arms, where she finally allowed herself to collapse and cry until his uniform shirt was damp.

"I don't know what's wrong with me." Connor finally lifted her head and sniffled resolutely.

"Really."

"I'm just overtired or something."

Jake rubbed the back of her neck softly. "Or something, Haus."

Connor was beyond relieved to have the uninterrupted time between calls to sit in the McDonald's parking lot with Jake and cry. Still, she had to find a way to pull it together. The radio wouldn't stay quiet for long.

As if on queue, the speaker on the dash crackled and a tone rang out. And not 884's tone, either. No. This was a tone Connor had heard only one other time—one year earlier, when the bombs exploded at the finish line of the Boston Marathon. This was an SOS. A distress signal to every EMS, BFD, and officer with a radio. Her throat clenched and she instinctively leaned forward.

"All units, be advised we have word of a hostage situation at Dorchester High School."

"What?" Jake's voice trembled.

"Shhh."

"Reports right now have PD on scene, but the shooter's still armed and inside. We have no idea how many victims there are at this time."

Connor's throat tightened harder.

"Also, all units be advised there is an engine company inside the building. We will keep you posted when we know more. Please do not respond to the scene unless requested."

"Engine company? What does he mean, Jake?" Connor looked at Jake desperately, but he was motionless and pale. "Jake! What's going on?"

"It's them."

"Who, Jake?!"

"Taylor! And Ace! And…Logan. Logan's in there, Haus."

The world stopped. Time stopped. Or at least it didn't matter anymore. Not to Connor. And the all-too-familiar feeling of loss once again gripped her, threatening to take her with it, once and for all.

"What do you mean, they're in there?" Connor finally said, the duck inside of her peeking its head out just a little.

"Their engine was doing a career day at the high school. Taylor told me this morning."

She could see Jake's heart through his shirt as he swallowed back tears. This couldn't be happening. Not again.

"And Logan's with them? You're sure?" Connor shook.

"Yes. I'm sure."

"Let's go."

"Where?!"

"Dorchester. I need to make sure she's okay."

"But they said…"

"I don't care what they said! I'm not losing anyone else I… Just drive, Jake."

Jake nodded once and slammed the truck into gear, peeling out of the parking lot and toward the high school.

❖

They pulled up a few minutes later to a sea of emergency vehicles and news vans so deep they couldn't get anywhere near the school.

"Shit." It took Connor only a second before she grabbed the first-in bag and took off on foot toward ground zero.

"Haus! What are you doing?" Jake shouted after her.

"I'm getting Logan out of there!"

"Good for you, Haus. Good for you," she heard him yell from behind her.

It didn't take long before Connor reached an officer standing in front of the police barricade, his face stern and unforgiving.

"I'm a medic. I need to get in there."

"Not happening. Scene isn't cleared yet. Shooter's still inside."

"There are dying kids in there! And firefighters! You want that blood on your hands, Officer? Or are you going to let me through?" Connor did her best to stand tall, but her knees quaked.

The officer took a deep breath. "Look, ma'am, I'd like to let you in there. But I have orders from my lieutenant. It's just not safe. I can't have you become a victim too."

Rule number one of EMS: don't let yourself become a patient. Connor knew this. She knew the risk. But she couldn't just wait it out with the others. She hadn't been able to save Kam. But maybe she could save Logan.

"I'm sorry," Connor said, timidly.

"No need to apologize. We're all just doing our jobs." The officer smiled cordially.

"No. Not for that…" Connor repositioned the bag on her shoulder. "For this." She pushed past him and sprinted toward the door of the school, not looking up again until she was inside. A gunshot rattled the glass behind her and sent her facedown on the ground, crawling under the bleachers in the gymnasium where she'd entered. She heard a quick, piercing scream from down the hall and then a nauseating silence.

"Where are you, Logan?" she mumbled to herself, inching along the wood floor toward the exit. Connor stood up and looked at herself. She had no weapon. She had no training. All she had was the unyielding will to get to Logan and save her—to make sure she got to see her face again. And all at once, everything about Logan that had frightened and confused her came quickly into focus. This was what she felt every day. And Connor had dismissed her because of the single greatest thing about her.

Another gunshot echoed and Connor fought the urge to vomit. But she kept going, running from one corner to the next until she got close to where the screams were coming from. One more shot, and one more scream—Logan's scream this time. She wasn't sure how she knew; she just did. And the nausea that had settled in her stomach transformed into a painful wrench. She couldn't lose her. Not now.

"Logan…" Connor whispered her name over and over, wanting to shout it as loud as she could as she crept through the halls of the school.

"Connor?" Logan's voice was weak and frightened. It was coming from right behind her. Before Connor could react, Logan's hand wrapped around her mouth. "Don't say anything else. He'll hear you."

Connor could taste the blood on Logan's hand. She just wasn't sure whose it was. Logan pulled her into a supply closet and locked the door.

"Oh my God, you're alive!" Connor collapsed against Logan's chest and wrapped her arms around her, savoring Logan's warmth and her smell and her strength she thought she'd never have again.

"What the hell are you doing here?" Logan pulled away and looked hard into Connor's eyes.

"I couldn't let anything happen to you."

"I'm okay. Really. Aside from being furious at you for coming in here like this."

"Oh, hypocrisy at its finest." Connor put her hands on Logan's shoulders and smiled, thinking now that she had her, she couldn't possibly let her go again.

"Stay here."

"What? No!"

"Connor. There's a girl out there. Her name is Becky. He shot her in the abdomen. I have to go back and get her."

"No. No, Logan!" Connor pumped her fists into Logan's chest, tears threatening to break through at any second. "They're coming soon. Just please, stay. I need you."

"She's going to bleed out, Connor. You know I can't do that."

Connor thought back to how she'd gotten there, crouched in a closet hiding behind half-full paint buckets and gym mats. She saw Kam running toward the burning car, and she tried to imagine a reality where she'd just let those people die. She saw a future with Logan—a forever she hadn't been allowed to have with Kam. Saving others was at Kam's core. It was in her soul. And Logan was no different. It was what she'd loved them for. Both of them.

"I know. But I'm coming with you."

"Absolutely not!"

"You might need to save everybody else, Logan, but someone needs to save you." She kissed her sweetly on the cheek.

"Let's go." Logan held her for a second longer, selfishly grateful Connor was unwilling to leave her side.

❖

Logan gripped Connor's hand as they silently made their way through the corridor toward where Logan had left the young girl when she'd heard Connor's voice. The only thing worse than losing a stranger would be losing Connor, and neither option was acceptable to Logan. The halls held an eerie silence. Backpacks and homework papers were scattered on the ground where they'd been left in a hurry, and lockers were still wide open. The fluorescent lights overhead were blazing, and a streak of blood faded around the corner and disappeared. Connor looked at her knowingly. Even Logan couldn't save them all.

"She's in that classroom there," Logan whispered.

"What if he's in there?"

"He's not. He thinks she's already dead."

"Then where is he?"

"I don't know."

Logan glanced up either end of the hall, took Connor's hand again, and dashed toward the classroom where Becky lay in a pool of her own blood, the color vacant from her face and a glassy reflection over her pale-blue eyes.

"We're here, Becky. This is Connor. She's a paramedic too. You're going to be okay."

The girl gave a strained smile and clenched her stomach, where her green T-shirt was now soaked in a damp red. Connor rushed to her side, taking her pulse on her wrists and neck, listening to the rattling of her breathing and looking for other wounds.

"Best guess, I'd say she's lost at least two liters already. She's tachy at about 140 and I can hear rales from here. We need to get her out of here," Connor said quietly.

"Don't touch her." A deep, unearthly voice rumbled behind them, one that didn't fit with the tall, slender boy it came out of. Both Connor and Logan lifted their hands over their heads as the boy pointed the barrel of his rifle first at one, then the other.

"Okay." Logan's heart beat so quickly it was buzzing in her chest, and she thought about losing Connor. And suddenly, she felt nothing but stupid for all of the times she'd insisted on risking her life to be a hero. Now, she was going to die. She could handle that part. In fact, Logan had come to grips with her own mortality a long time ago. It was hard to be a firefighter and not. What she hadn't come to terms with was Connor's death. No. That was something she would never accept.

"Let them go, and I'll stay. Shoot me instead." Logan choked down a lump in her throat. The boy with the rifle just stared at them, his eyes cold and dead, like they were all about to be.

"Logan, no!" Connor gasped and shoved her body in front of Logan's.

"What are you doing?" Logan snapped.

"I lost Kam. I'm not going to lose you too. I'm not going to lose one more person I...love."

For just a moment, their eyes locked and they were transported out of the hellish scene with the sadistic gunman and the proximity of death. And Logan was more determined than ever to keep Connor alive.

"That's sweet. But none of you are getting out of here alive. Sorry."

Becky let out a petrified scream and Connor closed her eyes tight, as if she were preparing to say good-bye, preparing to die.

"Freeze! Drop the weapon and put your hands up!"

Logan watched as a SWAT team crept around the bend, their guns aimed at the boy and their faces bearing hope. No one breathed as the boy stood motionless, then finally lowered his rifle to the ground and put his hands in the air. Before the SWAT team could even make it to him, Logan had grabbed the gun with the heel of her boot and kicked it away. In another instant, the boy was down on his knees, his hands cuffed behind him, and Logan was holding Connor, stroking her hair, her face, her skin—anything she could touch. She had to know Connor was still there. And that she was too.

## CHAPTER TWENTY-ONE

"Well, well, well. Big surprise. Logan Curtis the Fucking Hero." The BFD's lieutenant was waiting with the police commissioner when Connor and Logan emerged from the building. But this time, he was smiling at her.

"Sir…"

"Save it, Logan. I know your type."

"But I…"

The lieutenant clapped her on the shoulder and laughed. "Nice work. You saved that girl's life. And that little tip-off you gave us zeroed the team right in on the shooter. I'm proud of you. Even if you are a cowboy."

"Thank you, sir." Logan smiled, the humility that looked so good on her painting her face.

"What tip-off?" Connor asked as they walked away.

"I sent Taylor a text when we were in the closet. I was pretty sure I knew where the shooter was going to be."

"You knew the shooter was nearby and you let me come with you anyway?" Connor scoffed and tried her best to look angry.

"Oh, please. Nobody 'lets' Connor Haus do anything."

Connor's frown slowly crept into a smile, until she was laughing.

"You're right about that." She stepped toward Logan and put her mouth just inches from hers. "But right now, I think I'm going to let you kiss me."

Logan did as she was told, putting her strong hands on Connor's cheeks and pulling her in, kissing her softly until the world around them floated away.

"Just one last thing," Logan said.

"What?"

"You love me, do you?"

Connor smiled and took Logan's hands in hers. The scene around them was chaos. Police cars lined the parking lot, lights flashing, and reporters huddled near the barricades trying to get a glimpse of the shooter being hauled away by a team of FBI. Taylor and Ace sat on the back of Connor's rig with Jake, looking white as bed sheets. But all Connor could see was Logan, standing in front of her, strong and brave and foolish and perfect.

"I love you."

Logan's lips curled into the biggest, proudest smile Connor had ever seen on her. And that was saying a lot.

"You do?"

"Yes. Are you going to make me keep saying it?" Connor laughed.

"Maybe just one more time."

"I'm in love with you, Logan Curtis. Hell, I probably have been since your lug-of-a-firefighter ass spilled coffee on me in the Boston City cafeteria that day. And yes, you terrify me. And yes, the fact that you've almost died at least three times since I've known you does little to help that. But I'll be damned if I'll let that happen. Even if it means I have to keep running in after you. I'll do it. Indefinitely."

Logan's smile grew until her bold eyes dampened just slightly, and she wrapped her arms around Connor again.

"But wait…"

Logan pulled away again and Connor fought back a shudder. She didn't want to wait anymore. She'd been waiting forever for Logan.

"What?"

"None of this changes the last conversation we had, Connor. You said you weren't ready to move on."

Connor nuzzled her head under Logan's chin and stayed there, warm and safe.

"No. You said that. You never gave me a chance to say otherwise."

"But...Kam..."

"Kam was Kam. And I will always love her. But she wanted me to be happy. And you, Logan...You make me happy. I love you. My memories of Kam, and my love for you, those two things aren't mutually exclusive."

"So you are ready to love me then?" Logan asked softly.

"More than ready."

"Let's get out of here."

Connor smiled, amazed at how much peace she could find in the middle of bedlam—peace she got from Logan. "Only if you're coming with me."

Logan kissed her again.

"Always."

❖

It wasn't until they made it back to Connor's apartment that she felt like she could actually begin to breathe again. Logan was safe. And she was there, with her.

"I've never needed a shower so badly in my life," Logan said, stripping down to her boxers and bra and immediately tying her stained clothes up in a plastic shopping bag.

"After today, I don't want to let you out of my sight for even long enough to do that."

Logan moved to her and pressed her nearly naked body against Connor's. Connor shook with need, wondering how she'd managed to shut her out for so long. Not when this felt so right.

"Just promise me you'll be right here when I get out."

"Right here."

Logan turned the water up until it was nearly scalding and let it beat on her shoulders and neck and back. She'd nearly died today. That had never bothered her before. But this time, it was different. This time, she had Connor to think about. She had Connor to come home to.

She walked out of the shower, where Connor was waiting in bed, only a thin sheet covering her.

"I told you I'd be here when you got out," Connor said, a coy smile taking over her soft features. "Now come here."

Logan let her towel fall to the floor, walked slowly to the bed, and climbed in next to her.

"You are terribly bossy. Did you know that, Paramedic Haus?"

Connor moved her body on top of Logan's and kissed her mouth, then her ear and down to her neck, until Logan's breath was hot and fast. She looked at Logan, her face suddenly grave.

"What is it?" Logan asked, alarmed.

"I love you." She smiled tenderly.

"I love you too, Connor. You know I do." She cradled Connor's face in her hands and kissed her, gently at first, and then with a growing need that seemed to have been building for years—maybe even more.

Connor awoke just after dawn, the early spring sunlight streaming in through the bedroom blinds. She warmed from the inside, all the way to her fingers, as she turned around and looked into Logan's sleeping face. A small, quiet sigh escaped her lips, and Connor smiled. She was alive. And she was here with Logan. Connor couldn't help but wonder how she'd let so much time pass her by without letting Logan in. Without letting her love her. It didn't matter. She was here now. They had time left.

Suddenly unsettled, Connor leaned over, carefully kissed the scar on Logan's shoulder, and slowly uncovered herself. She made her way to the living room and stared at the coat rack for a long time, where Kam's bunker gear still hung, waiting. She and Logan had time for a long life together. But she didn't have time to live in the past. Kam wouldn't have wanted it. And she didn't want it anymore.

It was time.

Connor reached up, took down the jacket and helmet, and folded them carefully. And as one last tear hit the floor, she placed them in a box, slid it into the closet, and closed the door.

# About the Author

Emily Smith was born and raised in a small town, where she started writing at an early age. She graduated from the University of New Hampshire with a BA in English and went on to publish her first book, *Searching For Forever*, which pulled her headfirst into the world of creative writing. After years of working in medicine, Emily is currently in school becoming a physician assistant. She lives in Boston with her wife, Jillian; their dog, Rudy; and their cat, Cecilia.

# Books Available from Bold Strokes Books

**24/7** by Yolanda Wallace. When the trip of a lifetime becomes a pitched battle between life and death, will anyone survive? (978-1-62639-6-197)

**A Return to Arms** by Sheree Greer. When a police shooting makes national headlines, activists Folami and Toya struggle to balance their relationship and political allegiances, a struggle intensified after a fiery young artist enters their lives. (978-1-62639-6-814)

**After the Fire** by Emily Smith. Paramedic Connor Haus is convinced her time for love has come and gone, but when firefighter Logan Curtis comes into town, she learns it may not be too late after all. (978-1-62639-6-524)

**Dian's Ghost** by Justine Saracen. The road to genocide is paved with good intentions. (978-1-62639-5-947)

**Fortunate Sum** by M. Ullrich. Financial advisor Catherine Carter lives a calculated life, but after a collision with spunky Imogene Harris (her latest client) and unsolicited predictions, Catherine finds herself facing an unexpected variable: Love. (978-1-62639-5-305)

**Soul to Keep** by Rebekah Weatherspoon. What *won't* a vampire do for love… (978-1-62639-6-166)

**When I Knew You** by KE Payne. Eight letters, three friends, two lovers, one secret. Can the past ever be forgiven? (978-1-62639-5-626)

**Wild Shores** by Radclyffe. Can two women on opposite sides of an oil spill find a way to save both a wildlife sanctuary and their hearts? (978-1-62639-6-456)

**Love on Tap** by Karis Walsh. Beer and romance are brewing for Tace Lomond when archaeologist Berit Katsaros comes into her life. (987-1-162639-564-0)

**Love on the Red Rocks** by Lisa Moreau. An unexpected romance at a lesbian resort forces Malley to face her greatest fears where she must choose between playing it safe or taking a chance at true happiness. (987-1-162639-660-9)

**Tracker and the Spy** by D. Jackson Leigh. There are lessons for all when Captain Tanisha is assigned untried pyro Kyle and a lovesick dragon horse for a mission to track the leader of a dangerous cult. (987-1-162639-448-3)

**Whirlwind Romance** by Kris Bryant. Will chasing the girl break Tristan's heart or give her something she's never had before? (987-1-162639-581-7)

**Whiskey Sunrise** by Missouri Vaun. Culture and religion collide when Lovey Porter, daughter of a local Baptist minister, falls for the handsome thrill-seeking moonshine runner, Royal Duval. (987-1-162639-519-0)

**Dyre: By Moon's Light** by Rachel E. Bailey. A young werewolf, Des, guards the aging leader of all the Packs: the Dyre. Stable employment—nice work, if you can get it…at least until silver bullets start to fly. (978-1-62639-6-623)

**Fragile Wings** by Rebecca S. Buck. In Roaring Twenties London, can Evelyn Hopkins find love with Jos Singleton or will the scars of the Great War crush her dreams? (978-1-62639-5-466)

**Live and Love Again** by Jan Gayle. Jessica Whitney could be Sarah Jarret's second chance at love, but their differences and Sarah's grief continue to come between their budding relationship. (978-1-62639-5-176)

**Starstruck** by Lesley Davis. Actress Cassidy Hayes and writer Aiden Darrow find out the hard way not all life-threatening drama is confined to the TV screen or the pages of a manuscript. (978-1-62639-5-237)

**Stealing Sunshine** by Tina Michele. Under the Central Florida sun, two women struggle between fear and love as a dangerous plot of deception and revenge threatens to steal priceless art and lives. (978-1-62639-4-452)

**The Fifth Gospel** by Michelle Grubb. Hiding a Vatican secret is dangerous—sharing the secret suicidal—can Felicity survive a perilous book tour, and will her PR specialist, Anna, be there when it's all over? (978-1-62639-4-476)

**Cold to the Touch** by Cari Hunter. A drug addict's murder is the start of a dangerous investigation for Detective Sanne Jensen and Dr. Meg Fielding, as they try to stop a killer with no conscience. (978-1-62639-526-8)

**Forsaken** by Laydin Michaels. The hunt for a killer teaches one woman that she must overcome her fear in order to love, and another that success is meaningless without happiness. (978-1-62639-481-0)

**Infiltration** by Jackie D. When a CIA breach is imminent, a Marine instructor must stop the attack while protecting her heart from being disarmed by a recruit. (978-1-62639-521-3)

**Midnight at the Orpheus** by Alyssa Linn Palmer. Two women desperate to make their way in the world, a man hell-bent on revenge, and a cop risking his career: all in a day's work in Capone's Chicago. (978-1-62639-607-4)

**Spirit of the Dance** by Mardi Alexander. Major Sorla Reardon's return to her family farm to heal threatens Riley Johnson's safe life when small-town secrets are revealed, and love may not conquer all. (978-1-62639-583-1)

**Sweet Hearts** by Melissa Brayden, Rachel Spangler, and Karis Walsh. Do you ever wonder *Whatever happened to...*? Find out when you reconnect with your favorite characters from Melissa Brayden's *Heart Block*, Rachel Spangler's *LoveLife*, and Karis Walsh's *Worth the Risk*. (978-1-62639-475-9)

**Totally Worth It** by Maggie Cummings. Who knew there's an all-lesbian condo community in the NYC suburbs? Join twentysomething BFFs Meg and Lexi at Bay West as they navigate friendships, love, and everything in between. (978-1-62639-512-1)

**Illicit Artifacts** by Stevie Mikayne. Her foster mother's death cracked open a secret world Jil never wanted to see…and now she has to pick up the stolen pieces. (978-1-62639-472-8)

**Pathfinder** by Gun Brooke. Heading for their new homeworld, Exodus's chief engineer Adina Vantressa and nurse Briar Lindemay carry game-changing secrets that may well cause them to lose everything when disaster strikes. (978-1-62639-444-5)

**Prescription for Love** by Radclyffe. Dr. Flannery Rivers finds herself attracted to the new ER chief, city girl Abigail Remy, and the incendiary mix of city and country, fire and ice, tradition and change is combustible. (978-1-62639-570-1)

**Ready or Not** by Melissa Brayden. Uptight Mallory Spencer finds relinquishing control to bartender Hope Sanders too tall an order in fast-paced New York City. (978-1-62639-443-8)

**Summer Passion** by MJ Williamz. Women loving women is forbidden in 1946 Hollywood, yet Jean and Maggie strive to keep their love alive and away from prying eyes. (978-1-62639-540-4)

**The Princess and the Prix** by Nell Stark. "Ugly duckling" Princess Alix of Monaco was resigned to loneliness until she met racecar driver Thalia d'Angelis. (978-1-62639-474-2)

**Winter's Harbor** by Aurora Rey. Lia Brooks isn't looking for love in Provincetown, but when she discovers chocolate croissants and pastry chef Alex McKinnon, her winter retreat quickly starts heating up. (978-1-62639-498-8)

**The Time Before Now** by Missouri Vaun. Vivian flees a disastrous affair, embarking on an epic, transformative journey to escape her past, until destiny introduces her to Ida, who helps her rediscover trust, love, and hope. (978-1-62639-446-9)

**Twisted Whispers** by Sheri Lewis Wohl. Betrayal, lies, and secrets—whispers of a friend lost to darkness. Can a reluctant psychic set things right or will an evil soul destroy those she loves? (978-1-62639-439-1)

**The Courage to Try** by C.A. Popovich. Finding love is worth getting past the fear of trying. (978-1-62639-528-2)

**Break Point** by Yolanda Wallace. In a world readying for war, can love find a way? (978-1-62639-568-8)

**Countdown** by Julie Cannon. Can two strong-willed, powerful women overcome their differences to save the lives of seven others and begin a life they never imagined together? (978-1-62639-471-1)

**Keep Hold** by Michelle Grubb. Claire knew some things should be left alone and some rules should never be broken, but the most forbidden, well, they are the most tempting. (978-1-62639-502-2)

**Deadly Medicine** by Jaime Maddox. Dr. Ward Thrasher's life is in turmoil. Her partner Jess left her, and her job puts her in the path of a murderous physician who has Jess in his sights. (978-1-62639-424-7)

**New Beginnings** by KC Richardson. Can the connection and attraction between Jordan Roberts and Kirsten Murphy be enough for Jordan to trust Kirsten with her heart? (978-1-62639-450-6)